DETROIT PUBLIC LIBRARY

3 5674 05434596 3

THE SERIAL

CHEATER

 663-1148- Cillian

A Novel By

Silk White

Good2Go Publishing

KNAPP BRANCH LIBRARY
13330 CONANT
DETROIT, MICHIGAN 48212
(313) 481-1772

KN
JUL 14'

Good2Go Publishing

All rights reserved, therefore no part of this book may be used or reproduced in any manner whatsoever without written permission expert in case of brief quotations embodied in critical articles or reviews. For more information, contact publisher.

This novel is a work of fiction. All the characters, organizations, establishments, and events portrayed in this novel are either product of the author's imagination or are fiction.

GOOD2GO PUBLISHING

7311 W. Glass Lane

Laveen, AZ 85339

Copyright © 2014 by Silk White

www.good2gopublishing.com

twitter @good2gobooks

G2G@good2gopublishing.com

Facebook.com/good2gopublishing

ThirdLane Marketing: Brian James

Brian@good2gopublishing.com

Cover design: Davida Baldwin

Editor: Kesha Buckhana

Typesetter: Harriet Wilson

ISBN: 9780996060912

Printed in the United States of America

10 9 6 7 6 5 4 3 2 1

BOOKS BY THIS AUTHOR

Married To Da Streets

Never Be The Same

Stranded

Tears of a Hustler

Tears of a Hustler 2

Tears of a Hustler 3

Tears of a Hustler 4

Tears of a Hustler 5

The Serial Cheater

The Teflon Queen

The Teflon Queen 2

The Teflon Queen 3

ACKNOWLEDGMENTS

To you reading this right now, thank you for stepping inside the bookstore, stopping by the library, or downloading a copy of The Serial Cheater. I hope you have enjoyed this read from top to bottom. My goal is to get better and better with each story. I want to thank everyone for all their love and support. It is definitely appreciated!

Now without further ado Ladies and Gentleman, I give you "The Serial Cheater". ENJOY!!!

$iLK WHitE

THE SERIAL CHEATER

UP TO NO GOOD

Yolanda laid lazily across the sofa enjoying a glass of wine while one of her favorite reality shows played on the 70 inch 3-D flat screen that hung right above the fire place on the wall. As she sat enjoying her show, she heard her cell phone vibrating on the arm of the sofa. Yolanda glanced down at the screen and the word, "Unavailable" flashed across the screen. Someone had been calling her cell phone for the past week from an unavailable number, but she *never* answered unavailable/blocked calls or numbers she didn't know or recognize, but tonight her curiosity had gotten the best of her.

"Yeah," Yolanda answered with an attitude. She hated when people took time to block their number. That was the stupidest thing in the world to her. If you were brave enough to call, then be brave enough to show your number.

"Bitch when I catch you, that's word to my mother I'm going to cut your face," the woman's voice on the other end of the phone spat.

"Yeah I know tough guy," Yolanda yawned. If it was one thing she hated it was a phone thug.

"The next time Cam tells me that you over there stressing him out, I'mma show you what time it is," the woman spat. "The only reason I ain't wash you up yet is cause Cam has been begging me not to, but my patience is running real thin."

"Yeah I hear you talking."

"A'ight, stress my man out again bitch and watch what happen!" the woman threatened.

"You bum ass bitches kill me," Yolanda said. "It's funny how Cam is *your man*, but me and him live together and have been together for seven years. The last time I checked, I was the one with a 2 carat diamond ring on my finger. What do you have on your finger?"

"Bitch if you keep stressing my man out, you gonna have a ring around your motherfucking eye!" the woman spat. That last ring comment caught a vein and pissed the caller off. Now she had to return the favor. "By the way, the next time you kiss Cam, just know you're tasting my pussy, bitch!" The woman let out a laugh and then hung up.

Yolanda tossed her phone down on the sofa and growled several curse words. If it wasn't one thing, it was another with Cam and these other women. Yolanda did her best to be everything Cam needed her to be, but no matter what she did, it was just never good enough. Yolanda couldn't figure out what she was doing wrong or what another woman could do for Cam that she couldn't. The more she tried to figure it out, the more complicated things became.

"Lord please give me the strength to deal with this man of mines," Yolanda said looking up at the ceiling. Yolanda played out several different ways she was going to curse Cam out when he got home in her head.

Cam was in the music business and a well-known famous manager and song writer. Whenever Yolanda harassed him about any other chicks, he used his *job* as an excuse, but tonight Yolanda wasn't going for none of that shit. Tonight she was going to put her foot down.

"I done had enough of this shit," Yolanda huffed as she stomped over to the wet bar area in the house and refilled her glass with more wine. Yolanda favored the actress Stacey Dash except she was

about twenty five to thirty pounds heavier. She weighed 170 lbs but she carried it all in her hips, ass, and thighs. Yolanda walked around the house barefoot. A purple bra and thong set was the only thing that covered her body. She rarely wore clothes while in the house. Yolanda downed her drink and quietly refilled her glass when she heard the locks on the front door being unlocked.

Cam walked through the front door with a look on his face that said he had been drinking. He had on a pair of red high top Prada sneakers, black jeans, and a black tight fitting T-shirt. Over top of his T-shirt he sported a tight fitting red leather motorcycle jacket. He wore two chains hanging from his neck and a pair of dark shades covered his eyes. "What's up baby?" he said with a smile. Just from the look on Yolanda's face he could tell that she was mad with him about something. Cam walked over to Yolanda and leaned in for a kiss. Yolanda blocked his attempt with a firm hand to the chest. "Don't what's up baby me" she hissed looking at Cam from head to toe. "I don't know where your mouth has been."

"Damn you going to play me like that?" Cam asked licking his lips as he took in all of his woman's sexiness. "I been out working all day and I can't get a kiss?"

"One of your bitches called my phone again today threatening me," Yolanda huffed with her arms folded across her chest. "If you going to fuck around on me, the least you can do is keep your bitches in check."

"What bitches you talking about baby?" Cam said faking ignorance. Everyone knew Cam couldn't help himself when it came to women. He had a problem that needed professional help to be fixed. Cam lifted Yolanda's hand up so she could see the diamond ring on her finger. "You are my queen. You and not no one else. You never forget that you hear me?"

Yolanda nodded her head and whispered, "Yes."

"Yes what?"

"Yes daddy," Yolanda said.

Cam pulled her in close for a hug. "Come on baby, you know I love you to death and I know a lot of women be in my face, but that's only cause they see my face on T.V. all the time. I swear to God I don't be fucking with all these women on some personal shit. It's just business," he lied with straight face. "I brought this big ass house for us, not no other chicks. When you see me on T.V. with them video hoes that's all for T.V. and I'm just acting baby. Nothing more, nothing less," he said convincingly. In the middle of his pitch, Cam's phone began ringing. He smoothly reached down and hit the ignore button on his new Galaxy phone and prayed that Yolanda didn't make anything of it.

"Cameron you're a song writer and manager so I don't understand why you have to be all up in videos dancing and popping bottles. Shouldn't you be behind the scenes?" Yolanda asked.

"I'm not a behind the scenes type of nigga," Cam said arrogantly as the phone on his hip began to ring again, and again he hit the ignore button.

Yolanda's eye went from the phone on Cam's hip up to his face. "You not gonna answer that?" she asked with a raised brow. "You see that's the shit I be talking about. You always…"

Before Yolanda could say another word Cam grabbed her and shoved his tongue in her mouth. He went from Yolanda's lips down to her neck as he jammed his hand down the front of Yolanda's thong and began flicking his fingers across her clit in a rapid motion. "What I told you about worrying about stupid shit?" Cam growled through clench teeth as her wetness covered his fingers. "Huh?"

"I'm sorry daddy," Yolanda moaned as she felt herself cream on Cam's fingers.

"Get down on your knees!" Cam ordered as he watched Yolanda do as she was told. He then un-did his pants and pulled out his already hard dick and waved it in front of Yolanda's face. He watched as her eyes followed his dick as if she was being hypnotized. "Who dick is this!?"

"My dick," Yolanda answered.

"I can't hear you!"

"My dick!" Yolanda purred in a strong sexually charged voice.

"Show me," he said and then jammed his dick in Yolanda's mouth with force.

"Mmmmm," Yolanda moaned as she went to work. A tremor went through Cam as Yolanda took all of him in her throat and tickled his balls with her tongue. Yolanda began to work him expertly with her mouth, locking her thumb and index finger around his shaft. She began jerking his thick dick slowly. Yolanda began to suck him off at various speeds, spitting down the side of his shaft to keep it nice and slick.

Cam took a step back and made Yolanda bend and touch her toes as he entered her roughly from behind. He gripped Yolanda's waist tightly and fucked her like he had just been released from doing a ten year bid in prison.

"OH MY FUCKING GOD!!!" Yolanda held her breath for a moment, flared her nostrils, arched her back, and her legs tightened as she let out a loud moan mixed with pleasure and pain and she enjoyed every second of it. She could feel Cam's balls slapping against her clit with each stroke he delivered. Cam moved Yolanda into different positions, pleased her from different angles, desperate angles, angles that Yolanda didn't even know existed. He slipped out and Yolanda moaned and rushed him back inside. She grabbed his ass and pulled him in deeper. Her breathing was thick and hot just like it was between her legs. Yolanda threw the pussy back at Cam until finally he let out a loud roar and then collapsed on top of her.

Once Cam finished putting in work he walked over to the bathroom and took a quick shower. His night was just getting started. He didn't really want to have sex with Yolanda tonight, but he knew with him having to be out all night, after fucking her brains out she'd be a little easier to talk to and maybe she would take the news a little better.

Cam stepped out the bathroom with a towel draped around his waist and began fishing through his closet for something to wear. As he pulled out an outfit he heard Yolanda sarcastically clear her throat.

"Going somewhere?"

"Yeah I gotta head to the club tonight and handle some business," Cam said with his back to Yolanda. He didn't even have to see her face to know that she was pissed off.

"Word?" she said. "What club *we* going to tonight?"

"No, no, no," Cam said quickly. "*We* ain't going nowhere. I said I have to go to the club tonight and handle some business."

"And what kind of business you got to handle tonight?"

"Why?"

"Just curious," Yolanda answered. Whatever business Cam had to take care of nine times out of ten, it had to do with some bitches and Yolanda hated that every woman knew what it was like to be with *her* man. She tried not to be jealous, but the way Cam carried himself while he was out, not to mention his terrible track record made it hard for her to trust him. Yolanda loved Cam with every piece of her heart, but she deserved better and she knew she could find better.

"Honey got a walkthrough at that new club downtown tonight," Cam said over his shoulder. Honey was his most profitable artist that he had in his stable. She was a beautiful, sexy R&B singer with a beautiful strong voice and enough star power to take the both of them to the top. Honey was the hottest chick in the game at the moment and from what Yolanda had read from all the tabloids, Honey was a stone cold freak. And she didn't like or approve of her man working with such trash. In every video and magazine that Honey was featured in, she was always dressed like a stripper and quick to show off and flaunt the huge fake round ass that sat up on her back that she paid good money for.

"You and her sure have been real buddy, buddy lately," Yolanda huffed on her jealous shit. "Something you wanna tell me?"

"Ain't nothing to tell," Cam said and then shrugged.

"You fucked her?" Yolanda asked.

"What be going on in that brain of yours?" Cam asked, but never answered the question. "Is that what you think I be out doing?"

Yolanda said nothing.

Cam walked over and kissed Yolanda on the lips. "You have to trust me baby."

"Can I?" Yolanda asked. "Can I trust you Cam? Can I really trust you?"

"Of course you can baby," Cam said as the doorbell rung twice. "That's Honey. Come downstairs and say hi."

Yolanda looked at Cam like he was crazy. "I ain't got nothing to say to that bitch. She's your problem, not mines." She hugged Cam tightly and kissed him passionately. "I love you daddy! Be careful out there and I promise I'll be right here in the bed waiting for you when you get back."

"I love you too baby," Cam said and then went out the door.

Cam stepped outside and spotted Honey leaned up against the hood of her 745 BMW. She sported a tight fitting short red dress, an expensive pair of red open toe heels, and a strong coat of red lipstick completed her outfit. Her honey blonde hair sat up on top of her head in a bun and she had an annoyed look on her face.

"What's up baby?"

"Don't you what's up baby me," Honey snapped. "You got me waiting for you while you in there playing house with that whack ass hoe! Time is money!"

"Fuck is you talking about?" Cam said brushing Honey's comment off. Every time he was with Yolanda, Honey always had some slick shit to say about it. "Get in the car and let's go."

"Did you tell her about us?" Honey asked as she backed the BMW out of the driveway. "I mean does she even know that we've been fucking like rabbits?"

"I heard the club supposed to be popping tonight," Cam said changing the subject as he looked out the window. He wasn't in the mood for Honey and her bullshit tonight. If she didn't bring in as much money as she did, Cam would of been kicked her to the curb.

"Oh you wanna play?" Honey took her attention from off the road and glanced over at Cam. "Keep playing and you gon make me fuck that bitch up!" she barked. "I'm sick of these hoes thinking they can just be with *my man* like that's cool or something."

"When did I agree that I was *your man*?" Cam asked with a confused look on his face. "Cause I don't remember ever..."

"You agreed to be my man when you was fucking me and I was coming in your mouth!" Honey said cutting him off. "Stop playing with me."

For the rest of the ride Cam did his best to tune Honey out because she was really beginning to work his nerves. If she wanted to believe that she was his main chick then so be it.

Honey pulled her B.M.W. around the back of the club where a team of bouncers and security awaited her and Cam's arrival. Once inside the club, party goers and fans flocked towards Honey not giving her room to breathe.

Honey reached back and grabbed Cam's hand as the security pushed and shoved their way through the crowd. Everyone held out their smart phones and snapped pictures and recorded the superstar as she made her way to the roped off VIP area. Immediately several bottles of champagne were delivered to the VIP section. Five big security guards guarded the VIP area like their lives depended on it.

Cam sat back getting his sip on, while several cameras snapped in him and Honey's direction. Cam hated being directly in the spotlight, but it was either that or back to the trap; a place Cam promised himself that he'd never visit again. Cam thoughts were interrupted when security dashed across the VIP area and stopped three screaming fans that had jumped over the rope in hopes to touch Honey.

"I hate coming to these ratchet ass clubs," Honey huffed as if she wasn't as ratchet as they came. She downed her glass of champagne and quickly refilled her flute. "What you wanna do when we leave here?"

"I don't want you drinking too much tonight," Cam said knowing how ignorant and ratchet Honey became when she was drunk.

"I'm not no baby," Honey snapped. "I know how to control my liquor."

"I know, I'm just saying I don't want you getting too smacked tonight. You know how you get," Cam pointed out.

"Fuck you mean, you know how I get?" Honey huffed with her face crumbled up. "You see I ain't got time for your bullshit tonight," Honey spat as she got up and began dancing to the music that blared through the speakers.

Cam shook his head as he continued to get his sip on. As he sat chilling he noticed this light skin chick that he used to deal with a while back. He quickly got up and walked over to the rope that separated him from the *"regular"* people.

"Yo, Tiffany what you doing up in here?" Cam asked smiling.

"I heard you were supposed to be here tonight so I wanted to come out and show you some love," Tiffany said.

"Good looking. I appreciate that," Cam said as he openly checked Tiffany out. Cam's weakness was a woman with a big ass and a deep wet throat and Tiffany had both. "Lemme get your math so I can holla at you later."

"You sure your girl ain't gonna get mad?" Tiffany nodded over towards Honey. "Because you know I don't have a problem fucking a bitch up."

"Give me your number before I don't want it no more," Cam said arrogantly. As Tiffany wrote down her number Cam noticed Red storm inside the club with a huge entourage behind him. Red was a well known trouble maker and petty drug dealer. Everywhere he went, trouble was sure to follow. A few months ago Red and Cam had a few words because Red had tried to holla at Yolanda. He knew Yolanda and Cam were together, but he didn't care. Red only wanted Yolanda because he knew that she was with Cam. Before the two got a chance to get physical, a mutual friend stepped in and separated the two before things turned violent. Ever since that day neither man said another word to the other.

Just as Cam got Tiffany's number, Honey walked up making her presence be known. "Why you over here talking to this raga-muffin?" she spat looking down at Tiffany.

"She's just a friend. There's no need for name calling," Cam said. He could tell that Honey was now drunk. He did his best to keep her from getting drunk while out in public because he knew that there were cameras on her every second of the day and one wrong move could hurt or possibly end her career.

"Step off hoe!" Honey said to Tiffany and grabbed Cam's hand and led him back over towards the couch.

"Yo you can't go around talking to people like that," Cam lightly scolded. "These are the same people that buy your albums," he pointed out.

"Fuck that bitch!" Honey said loudly. "Tell that hoe to go find her own man and stay the fuck away from mines."

While Cam stood talking to Honey, he looked towards the entrance and spotted Yolanda heading towards the VIP section. One of the security guards yelled out asking was it okay to let Yolanda enter pass the VIP rope.

"Yeah she good," Cam said reluctantly.

"What the fuck is this bitch doing here!?" Honey snapped, ready to act a fool.

"Just chill for a second," Cam said as he stepped off to the side to talk to Yolanda.

"You don't look too happy to see me here," Yolanda said slyly.

"What you doing here?" Cam asked trying to hide his anger.

"I came to have a good time," Yolanda said throwing her arms in the air.

"Take yo ass home!" Cam growled. "I'm out here working. You can't just be popping up when you feel like it."

"Yeah I see what kind of work you in here doing," Yolanda said looking Honey up and down. "You so full of shit Cam!"

"Umm can I speak to you for a second?" Honey asked cutting into Cam and Yolanda's conversation.

"Yeah you can speak to him when I get done talking to him," Yolanda snapped.

"I wasn't talking to you," Honey capped back. "I was talking to my daddy," she said just to piss Yolanda off.

Yolanda turned and faced Cam. "This the type of woman you gonna let come in between your family? Before you had anything, I was there for you. We been together for over five years. Does that even mean anything to you?"

"This is just business baby," was Cam's response.

"That's your word Cam?" Yolanda asked looking into his eyes. "You gonna let this trashy two dollar hoe come in between us... Me and you?"

"We'll talk about it when I get home," Cam said.

"No we going to talk about this shit right now," Yolanda snapped. "It's either going to me or its going to be her." Yolanda folded her arms across her chest. "What's it going to be?"

Cam looked up and saw both Yolanda and Honey staring a hole through him. "Listen baby we'll talk about this at home."

Yolanda gave Cam a sad look. "Ain't nothing left to talk about," she said, turned, and exited the VIP section.

Cam felt bad for doing Yolanda like that. He really loved her, but at the same time he couldn't fuck up his money.

Honey tossed a drink in Cam's face before three big beefy security guards escorted her out of the VIP section.

"Fuck!" Cam cursed loudly. If it was up to him he would have kept both women and moved them in together and lived happily ever after, but he knew there was no way either one of them would ever go for that. Just as Cam got ready to go after Yolanda, he heard one of the security guards yell.

"Yo Cam is this nigga good?"

Cam looked up and saw his cousin Peanut standing there with a Corona in his hand. "Yeah he good."

It had been years since Cam had seen his cousin Peanut and out of all the times he decided to pop up now.

"Damn cousin what's good? I see you doing it real big out here," Peanut said with a big smile etched across his face.

"When you get out?"

"I got out this morning," Peanut said smiling. "I went to see ya moms and she told me you would be here tonight so I came out to holla at you. Oh yeah, ya moms said she needed to holla at you about something too."

"I'll holla at her tomorrow, but fuck all that what's good with you? How it feel to be a free man?" Cam asked pouring Peanut a drink.

"It feels good, but you already know I'm ready to get this money," Peanut said looking at Cam. "I see you brushing shoulders with some pretty big people."

"You already know," Cam said. He hated when people watched and tried to count his money. He really didn't fuck with Peanut like that, but just to keep the peace he tolerated his ignorant cousin. "So what's your plans now that you out?"

"I'mma get it how I live. You know that, but I ain't gonna lie I may need your help," Peanut said with a serious look on his face.

"What's on ya mind?" Immediately Cam regretted saying that.

"Hear me out before you say anything," Peanut began. "I see you hanging around a lot of celebrities lately. I was thinking that maybe you could give me the drop on a couple of these fake ass rap niggaz if you know what I mean."

"You want me to give you the drop on these rap niggaz and celebrities so you can rob them?"

"Don't worry I'mma break you off some of the bread," Peanut said quickly.

Cam removed his shades so Peanut could see his eyes and know that he was serious. "Listen I don't live like that no more.

Everything I do is legit now. I have worked too hard to let everything I worked hard for go swirling down the drain," he told him. "You just got out of jail. Why don't you sit down and chill and enjoy your freedom for a second."

"Niggaz ain't got time for all that," Peanut huffed. "I gotta get this money."

"There's a million ways to make money besides robbing niggaz," Cam pointed out.

"Let me find out you done made you a *little* money and now you forgot where you came from," Peanut said taking a shot at Cam. "Everybody can't make millions of dollars in the music industry. Some people gotta do what they know best, but I guess you wouldn't understand that *Mr. Super Star.*"

Cam hated when people spoke like it was a bad thing to be successful instead of just being happy for him. Most people hated and envied him because of his success and some of the good choices and investments he'd made. "Let's go grab something to eat and talk some more," he offered.

"Nah I'mma have to catch you next time super star," Peanut said eyeing Cam's jewels. "Came here with Red; don't want it to seem like I'm a flat leaver."

"Fuck you hanging with that clown Red for?" Cam asked. "Keep fucking with bozo's like that and you'll be back in jail in no time."

"I know super star," Peanut said standing to his feet. "Guess I'll see you around."

"Yeah I guess so," Cam said as he watched Peanut exit the VIP area with a grimy look on his face.

"Bum ass nigga," Cam said under his breath. He was beginning to not like people. It seemed like every other day someone was coming to him with their hand out and if he told them no, they acted as if he had committed the worst sin in the world.

Cam poured himself another drink when he noticed Yolanda over by the bar being harassed by some clown. After taking a closer look, Cam realized that the man talking to Yolanda was none other than Red.

"This nigga here," Cam said to himself as he hopped up and headed over towards the bar.

"SWEET NOTHINGS"

Yolanda sat at the bar sipping on a Long Island iced tea. She couldn't believe how Cam had acted and treated her tonight, especially in front of Honey. She thought about going back over to the VIP section and slapping the shit out of him, but decided against it due to the fact that she knew that there were camera's all over the place watching Cam and Honey's every move.

Financially Cam took care of his responsibilities, but when it came to being there for Yolanda emotionally that's where the problem came in at. A tap on Yolanda's shoulder interrupted her thoughts. She spun around on her bar stool and saw Red standing before her with a smile on his face.

"What's good love?" Red leaned over and kissed Yolanda on the cheek. "Long time no see. How you been?"

"Oh hey Red," Yolanda said caught off guard. "I been doing alright."

"As beautiful as you are and all you doing is alright?" Red said raising an eyebrow. "Still fucking with that clown Cam?"

Yolanda nodded her head yes.

"If you were my shorty you'd always be happy and nobody would be able to remove the huge smile from your face," Red told her. "I can look at you and see that you're not happy," he pointed out. "Why don't you come and see what it's like to fuck with a real nigga for once in your life?"

"Nah I'm good," Yolanda said dryly.

"How you good?" Red asked. "You in the club sitting alone at the bar looking like you about to cry, but you good?"

"I said I'm good," Yolanda snapped. Right now she didn't want to hear the bullshit that Red was talking about. She was more focused on figuring out how she was going to fix her and Cam's relationship and get it in a better space.

"You one of those silly ass bitches I see," Red said laughing. "But you know what, it's all good. Smuts like you come a dime a dozen!" He laughed and turned his back on Yolanda.

"Nigga yo mother is a smut!" she capped.

Red slowly spun around and tossed the drink that he held in his hand in her face.

SPLASH!

"Watch ya mouth bitch," Red growled. "I'm not that bitch ass nigga Cam! I'll put my foot up yo ass!"

Yolanda's natural reaction was to attack, but a stiff jab to the face stopped her dead in her tracks.

"Bitch you must be crazy!" Red barked as he raised his foot to stomp Yolanda's head into the floor, but before his foot could connect with Yolanda's face he was snuffed from behind. The impact from the punch caused Red to stumble back into the bar. Before he got a chance to react, a team of bouncers hemmed Red up and roughly escorted him out of the club.

"You a'ight?" Cam asked as he helped Yolanda back up to her feet.

"Yeah I'm good," she said feeling a little embarrassed. Once everything had calmed down, Cam and Yolanda made their way to the exit.

"How did you get here?" Cam asked as he felt his cell phone vibrate on his hip.

"I drove," Yolanda said strolling through the parking lot.

Cam glanced down at his cell phone and saw a naked picture of Honey. The caption read, *"Your pussy is excited. Get over here and calm her down."*

Cam slipped his phone back inside the case on his hip. "Listen baby, I got one more thing I have to handle tonight."

"What?" Yolanda said looking at Cam like he was crazy. "Can't it wait until tomorrow?"

"I'm sorry baby. It's an emergency," Cam lied.

"Pleeeeease," Yolanda begged.

"I'll be home in an hour I promise," Cam lied again.

"Okay," Yolanda said in a sad defeated tone as she slid behind the wheel of her grey Range Rover.

"Text me when you get in the house so I know you made it in safe." Cam bent down, stuck his head in the driver's window, and placed a soft kiss on Yolanda's lips.

Once Yolanda's Range Rover zipped out of the parking lot, Cam pulled out his cell phone and called a cab. He had a sexy ass super star diva waiting on him in a hotel room butt naked.

"LAST TIME TALKING

TO YOU"

The next day Cam spent the entire morning fucking the living shit out of Honey. Their freak show was put on hold when Honey had to leave and meet with some rapper who was interested in her featuring on his new single. Usually that was Cam's job to figure out and decide who Honey worked with, but today he allowed Honey to go alone because he had another issue that needed his immediate attention.

Cam borrowed Honey's sleek two door Benz to go pay his mom a visit. Last night at the club his cousin Peanut had told him that his mother really needed to see him.

Cam pulled the Benz up in front of the project building and let the engine die. He hated visiting his mother in the projects. He had offered to buy her a new house, but his deranged father refused to allow Cam to help them out.

Cam stepped foot in the lobby of his mother's building and immediately he was swarmed by a crowd of people while waiting for the elevator to arrive. He smiled and took as many pictures as he could, but for each picture he took, it seemed like four more people showed up.

"Okay, okay that's enough. I'll take more pictures later," Cam said to the crowd.

"That's that bullshit!" A man wearing a hoodie yelled out. "My shorty been standing here for ten minutes waiting to take a flick with you and now you just gonna leave?"

"Yo fam I said I'll be taking more pictures later," Cam told him. "Relax…"

"No nigga you relax!" the hooded man barked taking a step forward. "I'm tired y'all fake ass celebrity niggas coming through the hood like shit is sweet."

Cam thought about getting it on with the hooded man for a second, but quickly decided against it. Any negative press could jeopardize him and Honey's career and future. "You got it my nigga."

"Yeah I know I got it motherfucker!" the hooded man growled at Cam's departing back.

Cam disappeared in the staircase and took the steps until he reached the floor he was looking for. Once he was out the staircase, Cam walked down the narrow hallway until he reached his mother's door. Cam knocked on the door as he felt his cell phone vibrating on his hip. He glanced down at the screen and saw Yolanda's name flashing across it. He quickly hit the ignore button and put his phone away. He knew more than likely she was calling to fuss about him not coming home last night and at the moment Cam didn't feel like hearing that bullshit.

Just as Cam went to knock on the door again, he heard several locks being unlocked as his mother finally stuck her head out the door.

"Heeeey Cam," Mrs. Hunter beamed. She was more than happy to see her only son.

"Hey ma wassup?" Cam said leaning in for a hug.

"I'm so glad you came by. Come on in," Mrs. Hunter said stepping to the side so her son could enter the apartment. The first person Cam saw when he entered the apartment was his father Ricky sitting on a worn out couch with a bottle of Absolute in his hand and a mean look on his face.

"How you been?" Cam asked.

"I've been fine. Have a seat," Ricky said.

"Nah I'm not going to be here for long," Cam said. He and his father Ricky couldn't stand one another and both men did their best to stay away from the other.

"I saw Peanut last night and he told me that you wanted to see me."

"Yeah I just wanted to give you the heads up. I saw Peanut last night and he was hanging around a bunch of men that looked to be up to no good," Ms. Hunter told him. "I know he's always been jealous of you since y'all were kids and I just wanted you to keep a close eye on him."

"Thanks ma."

"No I'm serious. I got a bad vibe from him when I spoke to him last night." Mrs. Hunter said. "He ain't been out of jail an hour yet and he worried about where you at. All I'm saying is to be careful and watch your back."

As Cam sat back listening to his mother, he noticed a little bruise under her eye. "What happen to your eye?" he asked switching the subject.

"Oh this old thing," Mrs. Hunter said trying to down play the seriousness of the situation. "This ain't nothing. You hungry?"

Cam turned his attention on Ricky. "Yo, how long is this going to go on for? Huh?"

Ricky looked up and gave Cam a dirty look, but still remained silent.

"Hitting on a defenseless woman makes you feel tough?" Cam barked. He had been witnessing Ricky beat on his mother since he was a child and he was plain sick of it.

"Cameron calm down baby. It ain't that serious," Mrs. Hunter said trying to defuse the situation before things got out of hand.

"Nah fuck that!" Cam spat. "I'm tired of this motherfucker putting his hands on you!"

Ricky stood up from the couch, took a sip from his bottle, and looked at his son. "Bitch what I told you about talking to me like you crazy!?"

"I'm tired of you putting ya hands on my moms," Cam said while clapping his hands together. "You ain't got nothing else better to do?"

"Listen boy," Ricky said sitting down his bottle. "I done told you about talking to me! You a bitch and I don't talk to bitches! Now I'm not asking you, I'm telling you to get the fuck out my house right now before it be some shit up in here!" he warned.

"What you gonna do if I don't?" Cam challenged. "I ain't mommy. If you hit me, I'mma knock ya old ass out!"

"You a disrespectful little motherfucker," Ricky spat as he bent down and made sure that the laces on his sneakers were tied tight. "But I'm about to beat some sense into yo stupid ass!"

"Ricky please no," Mrs. Hunter said jumping in between the two men. "He's your son!"

Ricky violently grabbed Mrs. Hunter and shoved her down to the floor like she was a piece of trash. "Bitch get out my face! I don't have a son," he said as he looked up at Cam who stood before him. "You think you can whip my ass?"

"Don't put ya hands on mommy again and I ain't gonna tell you no more," Cam said as he helped his mother up off the floor.

"Let's take this shit outside and handle it like men," Ricky volunteered. "I'm bout to teach you a motherfucking lesson."

"Baby please don't," Mrs. Hunter pleaded looking over at Cam.

Cam quickly broke eye contact with his mother and exited the apartment with Ricky close on his heels. This was something that both men needed to get off their chest and it was long overdue. Their ill feelings and hate for one another had been going on for way too long. Today was the day that they would settle it once and for all.

Cam stepped foot out the building and noticed a small crowd lingering around waiting for him to make his exit.

"Where that fine ass bitch Honey at?!?" a man in the crowd yelled.

Cam ignored the ignorance as he watched Ricky come out of the building and head straight towards him.

As soon as Ricky was in arms reach, Cam threw a quick jab that landed in the middle of Ricky's forehead causing his head to snap back. "I told you to stop playing with me right?" he bark as he followed up with a sharp right hook.

Ricky faked high and went low as he grabbed Cam's legs and scooped him up high and then dumped him down on his head. Cam quickly spun his father over and landed on top of him like a UFC fighter. Cam didn't really want to hurt his father, but the old man was leaving him no choice. Cam rained down blow after blow on Ricky's exposed face, turning his once normal looking face into a bloody mess. He continued to unload on him until a few bystanders finally stepped in and separated the two men.

Cam hurried back to Honey's Benz and pulled away from the scene. During the fight Cam noticed several camera phones recording the entire incident. Right then and there he knew he had made a terrible decision in engaging in a street fight with his father.

***

Yolanda sat in the hot tub sipping on a glass of wine with an angry look on her face. Not only did Cam not come home last night, but he also hadn't been home all day and trying to reach him on his cell phone was like mission impossible. The more Yolanda thought about the situation, the angrier she found herself becoming. She loved Cam, but she hated the way he treated her. In the beginning Cam was the perfect gentleman. Before the money and fame, Cam was the type of man that any women would of loved to bring home to meet their mother, but that was a long time ago.

As Yolanda sat in the tub sipping on her wine, she heard her cell phone ring. She answered it without looking at the caller id assuming that it was Cam returning one of the hundred messages that she had left him.

"Hello?" she answered.

"Where the fuck my man at bitch!?" the caller spat.

"Oh my God! What do you want? You ain't got nothing better to do than play on peoples phones?" Yolanda huffed. Whoever the woman was who was calling her every night was beginning to piss her the fuck off.

"Listen Hoe! This my last time telling you to stay the fuck away from my man! You can't keep somebody who don't wanna be kept!

It's obvious that he wants to be with me and I'm not going to sit around and let you try to sabotage our relationship," the caller barked. "Stop blowing my man phone up Hoe!"

"Get a fucking life," Yolanda said and then hung up in the caller's ear. She vowed that whenever she bumped into the mystery caller, she would give her an ass whipping that she would never forget.

Just as Yolanda got ready to refill her glass, she heard her cell phone ringing again. She looked at the caller id this time and saw Cam's name flashing across the screen.

"Where the fuck you been all night!?" Yolanda yelled into the receiver.

"Yo, I'll be there in 15 minutes. Get dressed and I'll beep the horn when I'm out front," Cam said and then ended the call.

Yolanda quickly hopped out of the hot tub, dried off, and quickly proceeded to get dressed. She couldn't wait to give Cam a piece of her mind. She opened her closet and pulled out a navy blue dress that she had never worn before.

As Yolanda was putting on her makeup, she heard the sound of a car horn blowing. Yolanda ignored the horn and took her sweet time to finish getting ready. Cam had made Yolanda wait over 24 hours to hear from him and now she was returning the favor.

Fifteen minutes later, Yolanda stepped out the house looking flawless. She walked like a runway model until she reached the black shiny sleek Benz.

"Damn you had a nigga waiting forever," Cam complained as he backed out of the driveway like he had a reason to have an attitude. "What you been doing since the last time I saw you?" he asked as if she was the one that had spent the night out.

"I should be asking you the same question," Yolanda said turning to face Cam. "Where the fuck you been and what the fuck you been doing that you couldn't answer your phone or at least call me just to let me know that you were still breathing?"

"You hungry?" Cam asked pretending to be super focused on the road.

"Where the fuck you been all night and who's car is this?" Yolanda questioned.

"I told you last night that I had some *business* to handle" Cam replied.

"And whose car is this?"

"Honey's," Cam said in a light whisper. As soon as the answer left his lips, he knew that he would never hear the end of it.

"So you been with that bitch Honey all night and then you got the nerve to come pick me up in her car?" Yolanda asked with her face crumbled up. "You a trifling motherfucker!"

"What is you talking about?" Cam sighed. "If you gonna be fussing all night, I can drop you back off at the crib," he threatened.

"You out doing all types of shit with all types of women and then you got the nerve to be mad at me like I'm the one out here cheating," Yolanda yelled. "Take me back home! I don't even care! You gonna miss me when I'm gone!"

"You ain't going nowhere so shut up," Cam said as he parked the Benz in the parking lot of an expensive Italian restaurant. "Stop running your mouth and lets enjoy the night."

As the hostess escorted Cam and Yolanda to their table, Cam heard his cell phone ringing and quickly hit the ignore button.

"You look pretty tonight," Cam said as he took his seat across from Yolanda.

"Are you ever going to grow up and be a man?" Yolanda asked.

"I been a man," Cam said as his cell phone sounded off loudly again. Just as before, he glanced down at the screen and then hit the ignore button.

"You're not a man just cause you make money. A man is judged by..."

"Now niggaz wanna tell niggaz how to be a man," Cam said cutting Yolanda off. "Why don't you sit back and let *your man* handle things."

"I would if *my man* would handle things the right way," Yolanda countered. She was sick and tired of Cam and his childish ways.

A waitress with a huge ass, plenty of make up on her face, and a long blonde weave approaching the table interrupted the two's conversation.

"Are y'all ready to order?" blonde hair asked the couple as her eyes lingered on Cam a little longer. "Oh my God you're Cam," she said with a lot of excitement in her voice blushing from ear to ear. "I thought that was you, but I wasn't sure because I didn't see Honey with you. Oh my God this is crazy! Can I have your autograph?"

"I don't have no paper," Cam said smiling as he checked out the waitresses curves and he had to admit that she was definitely working with something.

"Here write it on this," the blonde hair waitress said as she removed a napkin from apron. "Oh my God you are even more sexy in person than on TV."

"You think so?" Cam said openly flirting with the waitress with the fat ass right in front of Yolanda.

"I know so," the waitress said licking her lips seductively.

Cam signed the napkin and then handed it back to the waitress. "Here you go baby. Make sure you keep that in a safe place."

"Oh don't worry I promise to keep this in a real safe place. I'm your biggest fan," the waitress said in a seductive tone.

"Um excuse me but we're ready to order now," Yolanda said with an attitude. She didn't know what it was, but something about the waitress seemed familiar to her from how she looked, down to the sound of her voice.

"I'm sorry ma'am what will you be having?" the waitress said putting on a fake smile.

"I'll have chicken Alfredo and a Cesar salad," Yolanda spat and then rolled her eyes. She hated that a thirsty chick would bend over backwards just to get noticed and gain attention by any means necessary.

"And what will you be having tonight love?" the waitress said turning her attention on Cam.

"I'll have the same thing that she had."

"Your wish is my command," blonde hair said, grabbed the menus, and then spun off with her big ass jiggling even in her work pants.

Cam was watching the waitress' ass as she walked away until Yolanda kicked him under the table.

"She got something that you ain't getting at home?" Yolanda huffed. "I suck and fuck you each and every way you ask of me. What am I doing wrong?"

"What's your problem now?" Cam said as if Yolanda was becoming an annoyance.

"You flirting with that waitress is my problem!"

"What? All I did was sign a little autograph. How was that flirting?"

"You called her baby," Yolanda barked.

"And?"

"And?" Yolanda echoed. "So what you call everybody baby now?"

"That's just how I talk," Cam smiled.

"You think this shit is funny?"

"What? I can't smile? Why?" Cam said while smiling again.

"Smile again and watch me smack the shit outta you," Yolanda warned.

"I'm sorry," Cam said as he pulled out his cell phone and began to read his text messages.

HONEY: Cam you better stop playing with me and answer ya motherfucking phone!

HONEY: And I swear to god you better not be with that bitch Yolanda either!

HONEY: You better call me in the next 5 min or else we bout to have a big problem!

CAM: Yea

HONEY: Fuck you mean yea...nigga why the fuck is you screening my motherfucking calls!?

CAM: What are you talking about I been busy...

HONEY: Busy doing what?

CAM: Busy minding my business

HONEY: Keep motherfucking playing with me!

CAM: I love you

HONEY: What time you coming home?

CAM: Yo I can't spend the night with you every night...

HONEY: You need to move in with me already and stop playing!

CAM: I'mma hit you later

"Damn do you have to be on your phone all day?" Yolanda complained. "I mean can we even have dinner without you being on that stupid phone?"

Cam shook his head and placed his phone on vibrate. As soon as he did that he felt the phone vibrate in his hand. He glanced at the screen and saw Honey's name flashing across the screen. He ignored it and stuck the phone down in his pocket.

"Damn I can't even talk to you without you being on that phone," Yolanda continued her rant.

"Okay the phone is away now what you wanna talk about?" Cam shook his head. He felt his phone vibrate in his pocket again, but he ignored it. "Is this how you going to act forever; cause if it is you need to let me know now?"

Just as Yolanda was about to reply, the blonde hair waitress returned to the table with Cam's food. "Here you go love," she said sitting a plate down in front of Cam. "Is there anything else I can do, I mean get for you?"

"Nah that will be all," Cam said smiling.

"Um excuse me," Yolanda cut in. "But did you forget about my food?"

"Oh yeah my bad," the waitress said and then turned on her heels and headed back towards the kitchen.

"You see that's the shit I be talking about!" Yolanda spat. "Bitch must want me to whip her ass!"

"You need to chill with all that ratchet shit," Cam said as he dug into his food.

"Ratchet?" Yolanda repeated. "This bitch smiling all up in your face, trying to brush her titties up against you and I'm the ratchet one?"

Cam shook his head with a disgusted look on his face as he continued to enjoy his meal.

"Damn you just gonna start eating without me? You couldn't wait until my food came out?"

Cam sighed loudly and slammed his fork down. "I try to be nice and take you out to dinner and you ain't stop fussing yet. If I knew you would be fussing all night, I would have taken one of my other bitches out to dinner instead."

"How dare you talk to me like that!?" Yolanda growled as she tossed her drink in Cam's face. "Fuck you Cam!" she yelled as she shot to her feet. "And when one of them bitches gives you a disease I hope your dick falls off!" Yolanda yelled and then stormed out of the restaurant.

Cam thought about going after Yolanda, but decided to just let her go. He was tired of her complaining and acting like a baby all the time. He needed a rider in his corner, not somebody that was going to complain about each and everything he did.

Cam's thoughts were interrupted when the blonde hair waitress returned to the table carrying Yolanda's plate.

"Where did your friend go?" she asked.

"Who cares," Cam said waving his hand in a dismissive gesture.

"She didn't look like your type anyway," the waitress said helping herself to a seat. "I know your type and she wasn't it."

"And what's my type?"

"Me," the waitress said smiling. "I told you I'm your biggest fan so please believe I know everything about you."

"What's your name again?"

"You can call me Blondie," the waitress told him.

"Let me get your number real quick before I get up out of here," Cam said as he pulled out his phone and stored Blondie's number in his phone.

"And you better call me too," Blondie said smiling as she got up and headed back towards the kitchen.

"I'mma tear that ass up," Cam said to himself as he watched Blondie disappear behind the double doors.

"LAUGH NOW, CRY LATER"

C am sat in the studio chopping it up with Honey as the two got drunk and discussed future plans and future money.

"I think we can make twelve million this year," Cam said doing the numbers in his head.

"Fuck that money," Honey said licking her lips seductively. "We been so busy lately that I haven't had time to get some of that dick."

"Stay focused…"

"Oh I am focused," Honey said as she sat her glass down and melted down to her knees and began to unzip Cam's jeans. Honey slipped her hand up under her miniskirt and began to play with her pussy.

"I wanna suck your dick so bad," Honey moaned when she finally got a hold of Cam's manhood.

Before Honey got a chance to get her lips on Cam's thick juicy dick, he stood up, grabbed her hair, and forced her head back so that she was looking up at him.

"First tell me how bad you wanna swallow this cum," Cam demanded.

"Oh my God Daddy! I wanna taste and swallow that cum so bad!!!"

"How bad?" Cam asked as he stroked himself right in front of Honey's face just to tease her.

"So bad Daddy... I promise I'm going to swallow every drop!"

"Beg me," Cam demanded as he continued to stroke himself.

"Please Daddy? Please can I suck your dick? Pllleeeeaaaaasssse" Honey begged looking up at Cam with a hungry look in her eyes.

"I can't hear you!"

"Please Daddy? Can I please suck your dick, please?" Honey pleaded as her mouth began to water at the site of Cam's nine inch dick.

Cam grabbed Honey's head and jammed his dick in her mouth. Honey obediently opened her mouth wide and tried to suck the skin off of Cam's dick. Cam moaned as Honey took him into her mouth.

She slid her lips slowly down his shaft and began to flick her tongue over the head as she stared up at Cam.

Cam firmly palmed the back of Honey's head and began to fuck her mouth savagely. "You like that? Huh? You like that don't you?" he asked speeding up his strokes. The sound of Honey gagging on his length only excited Cam even more.

"Mmm...hmmm," Honey moaned looking up at Cam as saliva escaped from her mouth and dripped down her chin and neck.

Honey began moaning loudly as she got into beast mode. She held the shaft of Cam's dick with one hand and began jerking it while she massaged his balls with her other. She leaned her head back and spit on Cam's dick.

"That's right you nasty bitch," Cam groaned as he looked down and watched Honey suck his dick like her life depended on it. Cam stroked Honey's mouth a few more times before he finally blew his wad and released himself down her throat. "Damn that shit was crazy!"

"Daddy your pussy misses you," Honey said in a desperate sexual tone. She hiked up her miniskirt, spread her legs wide, took two fingers and began to rub her clit in a circular motion.

Cam got down on one knee like he was about to propose to Honey, but instead he dove face first into her hot wet slice.

"Ahhhh yes Daddy!" Honey screamed. "Eat this pussy Daddy! That's right, eat this fat wet pussy!"

Honey grabbed the back of Cam's head and forced his face deeper into her cave while thrusting her hips trying to smother him. She bucked wildly as Cam laid down his tongue game. Just as Honey felt herself getting ready to explode, there was a loud forceful knock at the door.

Cam's head shot up from under Honey's skirt. "Who the fuck is that?" he asked out loud. Whoever it was had to be a close friend or damn near family since they made it pass Honey's team of security guards.

"Whoever the fuck it is, they have to wait cause I need to get my nut off first," Honey said with much attitude.

Cam ignored Honey and got up and headed for the door. "Yo pull ya skirt down," he called over his shoulder. Once Honey's clothing was situated he answered the door.

When Cam opened the door, there stood Yolanda on the other side.

"Hey baby wassup?" Cam said with a smile. "What you doing here?"

"I came to check up on you to make sure you were alright since you haven't been home in two days or returned any of my calls," Yolanda said giving Cam the side eye.

"My bad baby. I been out of town," he lied. "I just got back in town today. How'd you know I was here?"

"I always know how to find my man," Yolanda said with a sly grin. "So can I come in?"

"Yeah sure," Cam said stepping to the side so Yolanda could enter the studio. As soon as Yolanda entered the studio, she spotted Honey sitting in an expensive black leather looking office chair bare foot.

Even though Yolanda hated and couldn't stand Honey, because the hoe was trying to steal her man, she still spoke out of common courtesy. "Hey Honey."

"Mmm..hmm," Honey hummed and then swirled around in her chair giving Yolanda her back.

"So what you been up to?" Cam asked. He was in an awkward situation, but he had to play it cool.

"I miss you... Can you please come home tonight? I'm tired of sleeping in an empty bed every night."

"I'll be home tonight, but it might be a little late. We got some rapper who supposed to come through and do a collaboration with Honey so who knows when we'll be done."

"Mind if I stick around for a little while?"

"Nah, you know I be serious when it comes to my work," Cam said making up an excuse just so Yolanda couldn't stay.

* * *

"Please? I promise I won't say a word. I just want to be around my man," Yolanda pleaded. She then leaned in for a kiss and without hesitation Cam kissed her with Honey's pussy still fresh on his breath.

"I guess so," Cam shrugged. "But I'm telling you now I'm going to be busy."

"How long she going to be here for? We got shit to do!" Honey called out. She couldn't stand Yolanda's guts and in her mind the only reason Cam continued to put up with the pathetic bitch was because of how long they had been together and he was calling himself being loyal, but Honey knew that Cam's heart was really with her.

Cam made sure Yolanda was situated before giving his full attention to Honey. Honey pulled Cam over to the side and began to air him out in a voice barely above a whisper.

"What the fuck is that bitch doing here!?" Honey snapped. "I can't work with that bitch here. You know I already don't like her!"

"Chill the fuck out," Cam said in a smooth tone as he sipped on his glass of Vodka and orange juice. "You be worrying yourself about nothing."

"Nothing my ass! Cam stop playing with me cause you going to make me hurt that bitch," Honey threatened.

"Calm down. This rap nigga will be here soon. We gonna lay this track down and enjoy our night," Cam said in an attempt to smooth things out.

"And you coming home with me tonight Cam and I don't wanna hear no bullshit," Honey said in a matter of fact tone. "Play with me tonight if you want to and I'll whip you and that bitch ass!"

Before Cam had a chance to respond, a sharp knock at the door grabbed his attention. One of Honey's security guards stuck his head in the door.

"Are you expecting a rapper named Snow tonight?" the security guard asked.

"Yeah send him in," Cam yelled back. The night had started off crazy and he just wanted to get it over with as soon as possible.

Snow stepped foot in the studio with his six man entourage close on his heels. He wore all black with a heavy amount of jewelry. A black Brooklyn Nets hat sat backwards on his head and a pair of dark shades covered his eyes.

Each man in his entourage wore black t-shirts that had the letters M.O.E. etched across their chest. The letter stood for *Money Over Everything*.

Cam could tell off the bat that Snow and his crew weren't to be fucked with. He had worked with many of other rappers, but from the gate he could tell that this would be an experience that he wouldn't soon forget. He had seen Snow in the news for his involvement in several shooting, and assaults, and he just hoped everything played out smooth.

"Cam," he said extending his hand.

"Snow," Snow said as the two shook hands.

"So glad you could make it. I've heard a lot about you and I'm happy to finally get the chance to work with you," Cam said. "Big fan of your music."

"You already know," Snow said in an uninterested tone. He craned his neck so he could look over Cam's shoulder. "Oh wassup, now you can't speak?" he called out to Honey who stood over in the cut pouring herself a strong drink.

"Heeeeey Snow," Honey squealed as if the two had known each other for years. She walked over and gave Snow a tight seven second hug.

Immediately Cam felt himself becoming jealous at the site of Honey in another man's arms.

"Damn ma you smell mad good," Snow whispered in her ear before finally releasing her.

"Thank you," Honey blushed. She loved Cam and was loyal to him, but she would be lying to herself if she said that Snow wasn't as fine as they came. "Okay well let's get this started."

Cam was getting ready to go over and accompany Snow and Honey until he spotted a man from Snow's entourage over in the corner trying to holla at Yolanda. He quickly walked over to where Yolanda sat. "Fuck is you doing?" he asked standing over Yolanda.

"It's not what you thinking," Yolanda said quickly. "I told him that you were my man and he said he didn't care and sat down next to me anyway."

Cam's eyes landed on the man that sat next to Yolanda. "What's good? We got a problem over here?"

The man stood to his feet and smiled. "Oh shit you that guy that was fighting that old man on TMZ," he said laughing. "Check this out fam, my name is Trouble and if you don't want no trouble your best bet will be to step the fuck off." Trouble was an enormous trouble maker and he was well known for starting shit. He had a quick temper and an even quicker trigger finger. He got his fame from being Snow's right hand man.

"Stay away from my girl or else we going to have a misunderstanding." Cam spoke in a calm tone, but there was no denying the malice behind his words.

"Fuck you gonna do?" Trouble said calling his bluff. "I ain't want that whack ass washed up bitch anyway!"

Cam was about to steal on the big mouth punk until one of his security guards stepped in the middle of the two.

"He ain't worth it boss," the security guard said.

Cam nodded his head and turned his attention back to Yolanda. "Go home and I'll meet you there in about an hour."

"You promise you gonna come home tonight?" Yolanda asked. Giving Cam's track record she knew the chances of him coming home tonight were ten to one, but she loved him so she believed him.

"I got you," was Cam's reply. "Come on let me walk you downstairs to your car."

When the two made it out to the elevator Cam leaned in and hugged Yolanda tight and slipped his tongue into her mouth. Being away from home so long, he was really starting to miss her. "Baby listen, I know we haven't been on the best of terms, but I just want you to know that everything I do is for us. All the late night working and traveling is all for us."

"I know Cam. I would just like it if you would at least try to balance your work and your relationship a little better. I really be sitting in the house all day missing you and wondering what you're doing every second of the day. You are my entire life. I ain't never love nobody the way I love you."

Yolanda's words made Cam feel like a piece of shit. There he was out running the streets, doing him while Yolanda was in the crib waiting for him to come home.

"I promise I'm going to do better," Cam said as him and Yolanda stepped on the elevator.

"And I promise I'm going to do better too," she said as she hit the emergency stop button on the elevator, causing the cart to jerk.

"Fuck is you doing!?" Cam asked looking at her like she was crazy.

"Don't watch me, watch TV!" Yolanda dropped her purse to the ground and knelt on it so as not to scuff her knees on the concrete floor. She quickly unzipped Cam's pants and pulled out his dick. She circled her thumb and index finger around his shaft and stroked it gently while fondling his balls with her free hand. Yolanda leaned her head back and spit on Cam's dick. "You like that don't you," she said in a sexually charged voice as she wrapped her lips around Cam's dick, drawing a low hiss from him. Yolanda gagged over and over as she did her best to swallow Cam's dick whole. She slid it farther and farther into her mouth until his dick had completely disappeared and her tongue touched his balls. Yolanda slurped on Cam's dick one last time before hopping up off her knees and pressing the button on the elevator to continue on down to the lobby.

"Fuck is you doing!?" Cam asked with a confused look on his face and a rock hard dick.

"If I give you everything now, ain't no telling if you'll come home tonight or not," Yolanda said smiling as she put Cam's dick back in his pants. "There's plenty more where that came from. It's just on you how bad you want it. If you want it bad enough I guess I'll see you at home tonight."

"I'll definitely be home tonight," Cam said looking down at Yolanda ass.

"Can I ask you a question?" Yolanda asked looking Cam in his eyes. "You not really out here fucking Honey are you?"

Cam's eye ticked, but he kept his face even. "Absolutely not baby," he lied. "You know better than to be believing everything you hear."

"You right," Yolanda agreed. "If our relationship is going to work, I'm going to have to trust you." Deep down inside Yolanda wanted to trust and believe Cam, but something inside of her told her to just keep a close eye on him, just in case.

When the couple stepped outside, Cam spotted Peanut leaned up against a parked car flanked by two hard faced men who looked like they were up to no good.

"Cuzo what's goodie?" Peanut asked with a wicked smile on his face. "I didn't know you recorded in this studio."

"Yeah just working on this next single," Cam said. "But what brings you out this way?"

"Heard some big time rappers were supposed to be recording in this studio tonight and I was hoping maybe I could get an autograph or something," Peanut said as his eyes landed on Yolanda. "Hey Yolanda, long time no see," he said with lust in his eyes. "Come give me a hug girl, we family." There was something about the way he was running his hands up and down her back that made Yolanda feel violated so she pushed him away.

"I'mma go wait in the car," Yolanda said and quickly walked off.

"Talk to me," Cam said once Yolanda was gone. "What you really doing here?"

"A little birdie told me that, that fake ass rapper nigga Snow would be making an appearance here tonight and I didn't want to miss it. If you know what I mean?" Peanut told him.

"Come on Peanut. You can't come down here with that shit," Cam told him. "This is my job now."

"And this is my job," Peanut said lifting his shirt showing off the butt of a big hand gun. "A nigga gotta eat."

Cam pulled Peanut over to the side so the two could talk in private. "Listen, I ain't telling you what you can and can't do, but you gotta respect what I'm out here trying to do. You can't just be coming around here with guns and shit."

"If you ain't going to feed a nigga, then you can't tell a nigga how to eat," Peanut said eyeing the thick chain that hung around Cam's neck. "Everybody can't be a baller like you and have a chick that makes millions."

Immediately Peanut's words struck Cam as jealously and rubbed him the wrong way.

"I don't stop your paper so please don't stop mines," Peanut told Cam. "I'm getting this nigga Snow and that's that," he said and spun off.

***

When Cam made it back upstairs to the studio, he noticed Honey over in the cut with Snow reading over what he imagined was a verse or chorus. The rest of Snow's entourage sat around smoking, drinking, and talking loud.

As Cam made his way back over to Honey, Trouble stopped him in midstride.

"Yo, where shorty went? I was just about to hit that," Trouble said loudly drawing laughter from his cronies. Before Trouble knew what had happened, Cam had already snuffed him twice. He was going in for a third blow, but his security jumped in and separated the two.

Snow crept up on Cam from behind and stole on him. The impact from the blow put him on his back, but didn't put him out. Cam got prepared to block the onslaught of punches that he was sure to come next when he saw Honey take off one of her heels and began to beat Snow over his head with it like her shoe was a hammer.

"You must be crazy! Don't you ever put your hands on my man!" Honey yelled as security snatched her up off of Snow and hemmed her up against the wall.

Cam was glad when he saw his security escorting Snow and his entourage out of the studio. He was sure that Snow and his team were strapped and ready to go at the drop of a hat. Little did he know, but him and Honey had dodged a major bullet.

"You alright?" Cam asked looking over at Honey.

"Yeah I'm good. What was that all about?"

Before Cam got a chance to answer Honey the sound of rapid gunfire could be heard coming from downstairs. Right then and there Cam knew that things had just gone from bad to worse.

"LET ME GET THAT"

"**M**otherfucker lucky I didn't clap his ass," Trouble fumed as him, Snow, and the rest of the crew road down on the elevator.

Snow shook his head. It seemed like everywhere he went, his crew was always getting into some shit and every time some shit jumped off his name was dead smack in the middle of it. "Ya'll niggaz gonna have to chill with all that wild shit cause it's starting to fuck up money," Snow said looking around at his crew. "You know how much money we would have made from doing business with Honey?"

"It wasn't my fault," Trouble started to explain, but Snow waved his hand in a dismissive manner and silenced him.

"I'm about my money. If ya'll niggaz wanna run around gang banging and doing all this silly shit that ain't going to make no money, then ya'll can bounce," Snow said as the elevator reached the lobby.

As soon as the elevator door opened, a masked man with an angry voice jammed a gun in Snow's face.

"You already know what time it is you bitch ass nigga," Peanut growled as his two henchmen followed his lead and backed him up.

"Word? It's like that?" Snow mumbled. He looked around to check out his surroundings. He had never been robbed in his life and he didn't plan on starting today. "Listen you clowns don't know what you getting yourself into."

Without warning Peanut cracked Snow across the bridge of his nose with the hammer sending blood splashing all over the elevator walls. "Nigga this ain't one of your bullshit ass rap stories. This shit here nigga is real life," he said as he went to snatch Snow's diamond chain from around his neck.

Snow clutched his nose as the masked man removed Snow's chain from around his neck.

"The rest of ya'll niggaz run all that shit too and hurry up!" Peanut yelled out to the rest of Snow's crew. He then turned his attention back on Snow. "Fuck you standing there looking stupid for? Run that motherfucking bracelet!"

Snow reached down as if he was about to unsnap his bracelet and then without warning he lunged at the masked man and grabbed the gun.

"Fuck that these niggaz gonna have to kill me in this bitch" Snow said to himself as him and the gunman wrestled over the gun.

Once the fight broke out, the other two gunmen opened fire right there in the small elevator. As Snow and the gunman wrestled for the gun, it accidentally discharged several times.

Peanut violently slammed Snow's head up again the elevator wall repeatedly in an attempt to get him to release the weapon. After tussling with Snow for a couple of minutes he decided it was best that he escape with the diamond chain and his freedom. Peanut kneed Snow in his nuts and then turned and ran for the exit.

As Snow hunched over, he quickly snatched his 9mm from his waistband and fired off four shots in a rapid succession at Peanut's departing back. One of his shots found a home in the back of Peanut's thigh.

When Snow looked to his left he saw the two other gunmen laid out in a pool of their own blood along with three members from his own crew. Last but not least Snow spotted Trouble sitting on the floor clutching his stomach as blood seeped through the wound and down his fingers.

* * *

"I still got my chain," Trouble mumbled with an ignorant smile on his face as if losing his life instead of his chain was more important.

"You gonna be alright," Snow said trying to keep Trouble calm as he dialed 911. Immediately his mind began to wonder who could have sent the gunmen and how did the gunmen even know him and his crew would be there tonight... The first person that came to mind was Honey. *"That bitch set me up,"* he thought to himself as he began putting the pieces to the story together. *"That bitch Honey and her manager set me up."*

"You know it was that bitch and her manager that set us up right?" Trouble whispered looking up at Snow. "Nobody else knew we were gonna be here tonight."

"Yeah I know. Don't worry, I'mma take care of it," Snow said as the police and paramedics entered the lobby.

"OUT OF HAND"

E ver since the shooting took place at the studio Cam called himself staying under the radar. Lately he had been in the news or on TMZ for all the wrong reasons, but not today. Today he was locked away in a hotel room with a bottle of Ciroc and a woman with a banging body. Cam had turned his phone off because both Yolanda and Honey were blowing it up.

"You need another drink baby?" Blondie asked as she lay in the bed butt naked with a satisfied smile on her face. She was the waitress from the restaurant and all night she had been serving Cam her goodies.

"Yeah I wanna drink that pussy," Cam said as he pulled Blondie towards him by her toned legs until she was close enough for him to sink his teeth into. Yeah Cam felt bad for cheating on both Yolanda and Honey, but at the moment he was just living for today.

* * *

Cam dipped his head in between Blondie's legs and began to slowly and expertly lick her pussy. Cam took his time as he sucked all over her swollen clit while moaning loudly. Blondie grabbed the back of Cam's head and shoved it further down into her pussy.

"Yes, yes, don't stop, yeah eat this pussy baby," Blondie moaned. Each time she thruster her hips, she pushed Cam's head further down.

"Argh you bout to make me cum!" she yelled. Her body tensed up and she began to shake a bit as her orgasm took over.

Cam quickly flipped Blondie over onto her stomach and slapped her ass.

Slap!

"You know I like that rough shit," Blondie said smiling back at Cam as she got on all fours. "Bring me that dick!"

Cam smiled as he looked down at the huge brown ass hiked up in front of him. When he entered Blondie from behind, the heat of her vagina radiated through him. Cam started off with easy long strokes to begin with. He didn't want to give Blondie too much too early, but from how good her pussy was he could tell that this wasn't going to last very long. Once he felt like Blondie was broken in, Cam went to work. He shoved himself roughly inside Blondie's box and tried to pulverize her intestines. "Yeah bitch you going to take this dick!" Cam growled as he sped up his strokes. When he felt himself about to cum he quickly pulled out, snatched off the condom, positioned himself by Blondie's face, and shoved his dick in her awaiting mouth.

Blondie moaned loudly as she tried to suck the skin off of Cam's dick. Yeah she had just met him, but to her it felt like she had known him for years, especially since she was his biggest fan.

Cam fucked Blondie's face like an animal until he couldn't take it anymore. He removed his dick, took a step back, grunted, and released his load on her face. "aaarrrrrgh!!!"

"Oh yes! mmmmmm...," Blondie moaned as she closed her eyes and stuck out her tongue while warm cum splashed on her face and tongue.

"Oh shit," Cam groaned as he fell back on the bed and lay on his back staring up at the ceiling. His life was beginning to spiral out of control. His personal life and business life were starting to mix all together and the outcome was sure to be a disaster. Cam rolled over and looked at Blondie. "So what you bout to do?" he asked hinting that it was time for her to leave.

"I thought we were supposed to be hanging out today?" Blondie asked with a confused look on her face.

"Nah change of plans," Cam said. "I gotta go meet up with Honey and take care of something," he lied.

"Take care of what?" Blondie asked nosily. She hated the fact that Cam had to be around a beautiful woman like Honey all the time. There was a lot of temptation out there which meant that if Blondie expected to keep Cam then she would most definitely have to step her game up.

"Listen I ain't with all the questions and shit," Cam said as he got up and started getting dressed. "I'll holla at you later," he said coldly. He wanted Blondie to leave on her own, but it was like she wasn't getting the message.

"Can you give me a ride back to my crib?" Blondie asked with a hurt look on her face.

"Nah it's quiet," Cam said. "I just told you I had some shit to do."

Blondie wanted to break down into tears. She couldn't understand why Cam would treat his biggest fan like this. She was so excited about seeing Cam and spending time with him that when she left her apartment she forgot to bring any money with her which meant she had no clue on how she was going to get home.

"Um baby?"

"What is it?" Cam asked as if Blondie was becoming an annoyance. He had already gotten what he wanted from her so now he didn't have to be nice anymore.

"You think you can spare some cab fare, cause I left my purse at home by accident."

"Spare some cab fare?" Cam repeated loudly and then busted out laughing. "Bitch is you crazy?" He was about to let her have it when a loud knock at the door grabbed his attention. This wasn't a regular knock. It was the kind of knock that had POLICE written all over it.

Cam quickly turned and looked at Blondie. "Who you told you were going to be here?"

"Nobody," Blondie answered quickly.

As Cam made his way to the door he could hear a woman's voice on the other side of the door yelling.

"Open this motherfucking door right now Cam!"

Immediately Cam recognized the voice to belong to Yolanda. "Shit!" he cursed. The last thing he wanted was for Yolanda to catch him laid up in a hotel with the same waitress that had disrespected her the other night.

"Open this door right now, before I kick it down!" Yolanda threatened as her banging got louder and louder.

"Yo hold on," Cam called out as he turned and faced Blondie and mouthed the words, "Get dressed."

Cam and Blondie quickly began to get dressed when they heard what sounded like someone kicking the door. Cam walked over to the door and snatched it open. "Yo wassup?"

Yolanda pushed Cam out the way and stormed inside the room. As soon as her eyes landed on the waitress, her heart shattered into a million pieces. "Really Cam," she said looking up at him. "The waitress though... I mean is it that serious?"

"Listen baby it's not what you thinking," Cam said trying to come up with a quick lie off the top of his head. Before he could say another word, Yolanda had slapped him across the face and was trying to rake his eyes out. Cam quickly grabbed Yolanda and slammed her down on the bed in an attempt to restrain her.

"Yo calm down!"

"Get the fuck off me!" Yolanda yelled.

"Calm down first!"

"Motherfucker I am calm!" she growled.

When Cam let Yolanda up off the bed she immediately turned her attention on the blonde haired waitress. "And you bitch! You should be ashamed of yourself! You give good women like me an ugly reputation! Stop being a hoe and go find your own man, cause this here is my man and you can't have him, *AND* if I catch you around him again I'm going to hurt you!"

"If that's your man, then why is he laid up in a hotel with me?" Blondie capped back. "If you were handling your business, I would be out of business so don't get mad with me cause you can't control *YOUR MAN*! That ain't my problem!"

"Oh my God! It's you," Yolanda said squinting her eyes staring at Blondie as if she knew her from somewhere. "It's you!"

"Fuck is you talking bout?" Blondie asked.

"The one that's always calling my phone; it's you," Yolanda said as she smoothly slipped off her heels. "It's you!"

"You got me fucked up," Blondie capped back. "Ain't nobody calling your phone."

"I'll never forget that voice! It's you," Yolanda said lunging at Blondie and tackling her on the bed. The two women hit the bed hard and then slid down to the floor. Yolanda landed on top of Blondie and got off as many hits as she could before Cam finally stepped in and separated the two.

"Yo chill!" Cam yelled as he struggled to break up the cat fight. "Let her hair go!" he said as he had to physically remove Yolanda's fingers from Blondie's scalp. Seconds later hotel security came in and threw all three of them off the property.

When Cam made it downstairs once again he noticed several people with their cell phones stuck out recording him being escorted out of the hotel.

"Yo here take this and I'll call you later." Cam handed Blondie a hundred dollar bill and walked away from her like he had never seen her before a day in his life. Then he walked back over to Yolanda who stood leaned up against her Lexus crying her eyes out.

"Come here baby," he called out.

"I can't do this no more Cam. I just can't," Yolanda cried.

"What you mean you can't do this no more? It's us against the world," Cam said trying to sweet talk his way back in. "We are a team. What would I do without you?"

"Stop it with all your lies and bullshit!" Yolanda yelled. "Because if you cared anything about me, you wouldn't treat me like this. I shouldn't have to come and find you in a hotel room shacked up with the next bitch while I'm at home being a good woman patiently waiting for my man to come home and do right... It's just not fair!"

"How did you know I was here anyway?" Cam asked curiously. It seemed like every time he called himself being slick, Yolanda would always catch him right in the act.

"Cause your little waitress girlfriend posted y'all's every move on Facebook," Yolanda sobbed. "I can't fuck with you no more Cam!"

"You see now you talking stupid." Cam went in for a hug, but Yolanda stopped him with a firm hand to the chest.

"I'm serious," Yolanda said wiping her eyes. "I'm packing up all your shit. You can come by and get it in a week." She walked around to the driver side of her car, hopped in, and left Cam standing there looking stupid.

"Fuck it! I don't need that bitch anyway," Cam mumbled as he walked over to his car.

"PROBLEMS"

For the next two nights Cam called himself laying low. Him and Honey had been laid up in her mansion fucking like newlyweds and drinking their problems away. Cam looked over and saw Honey laid out across the super king sized water bed sleep with her mouth open. Cam got ready to wake her up when his phone buzzed notifying him that he had just received a text message. Cam glanced down at his phone and read the text.

PEANUT: Yo what's good nigga I been trying to call you. Hit my jack when you get a minute.

CAM: My bad I been mad busy what's good tho?

PEANUT: Some funny shit went down the other night after I saw you...

CAM: What happen?

PEANUT: Nigga don't play stupid with me, you know damn well what happened, you went back upstairs and told that faggot Snow and his ppls that me and my team was down there waiting for him.

CAM: Fuck is you talking about?

PEANUT: Nigga stop playing stupid, you went upstairs and ran your big mouth and now cause of that 2 of my homies is dead...I thought we was supposed to be family.

CAM: I don't know what you talking about Peanut you bugging right now

PEANUT: Nigga fuck you, you think you some big time nigga cuz you fucking a dirty hoe that just happens to be famous...nigga pls I'm bout to show you just how touchable you are! You better watch ya motherfucking back cuz I'm sending the goonz straight at ya fucking head faggot!

Cam looked down at his phone with a confused look on his face. He had no idea what Peanut was talking about. He would never set his cousin up or let someone get the drop on his family. *"That nigga bugging right now,"* Cam said to himself as he gently shook Honey. They had to do a walk through at a club in a few hours and he didn't want them to be late.

"Baby wake up," Cam whispered.

At first Honey didn't stir, but when she felt Cam planting soft kisses on the back of her neck, she squirmed a bit. "Stoppp baby," she moaned as she moved her ass closer towards Cam. Cam laid in the bed behind Honey and continued to kiss her neck as he slipped inside of her from behind.

Honey arched her back and pushed her ass against Cam so he could go deeper. She let out a slow whistle of wind as he hit her spot. When she got tired of the spooning position, she rolled him onto his back and mounted him and bounced up and down on his dick like a mad woman.

After their sex session Cam and Honey hopped in the back seat of the all black Escalade as their driver drove them out to the club.

"You know I love you right?" Honey said out of nowhere.

"You better."

"No I'm serious, and you know I'll always hold you down no matter what right?"

"Where's all this coming from?" Cam asked curiously. "What's going on?"

"Well I heard from a few friends of mine that Snow has been telling everyone that you set him up to get robbed and killed the other night at the studio and now he done put some money on your head," Honey told him.

"Fuck outta here," Cam said in disbelief. "You bullshitting right?"

"No daddy I wouldn't play about nothing like that," Honey went on. "My friends were telling me that Snow's cousin, some guy named The Prince works for some big drug queen pin named Pauleena and they have a bunch of shooters that's supposed to be out to collect that bounty."

"This is crazy," Cam said rubbing his hand across his waves. *"First Peanut and now Snow thinks I set them both up when all I was trying to do was make music,"* Cam said to himself.

"I went out and got us something." Honey reached into her purse and pulled out a black .380. "Here I brought two of them. One for you and one for me," she said handing him the gun.

"And what you going to do with your gun?" Cam laughed.

"Nigga please! If anybody tries to hurt my daddy; I'm going to kill them," Honey said seriously. "I don't play that shit!"

"You are a superstar baby. You can't be out shooting nobody."

"Fuck that!" Honey snapped. "And fuck my career! You are more important than a stupid career. I love you to death! If somebody wants to do something to you, then they gonna have to go through me first!"

When the Escalade pulled up to the side entrance of the club, Cam made sure his four man team of security formed a circle around him and Honey before entering the club.

As always, screaming fans did their best to try and touch and snap a picture of Honey and Cam. Honey smiled and waved at the crowd as her security team roughly pushed and shoved people making a path towards the VIP area.

As soon as Cam and Honey arrived in the VIP section, one of the club's promoters handed Honey a microphone.

"Are y'all ready to have some fun up in this bitch or what!?" Honey yelled into the mic. "I can't hear y'all!!!"

The crowd erupted with a loud cheer.

"A'ight, let's get this shit started DJ! Play my new shit!" Honey yelled into the mic. When the beat to her new song dropped, the crowd went crazy. Cam sat back and watched as the entire crowd recited every word to Honey's new song that had just dropped two days ago.

Honey slid down onto Cam's lap and kissed him passionately. "I love you to death. None of this would be possible if it wasn't for you," she yelled over the loud bass.

"Hush ya mouth. You are a gifted and talented artist," Cam encouraged. "The sky is the limit for you ma." Just as the words left his mouth, Cam spotted Peanut, Red, and a few other hard face men staring at him and Honey from the other side of the club. Peanut said something to a few goonz and the next thing you knew, Cam noticed three men who looked like they had nothing to live for head in his direction.

"Baby hold on a second. I think we got trouble coming our way," Cam said nodding towards the three men whose eyes looked like they were on some type of heavy drugs.

"Let them motherfuckers act stupid if they want to," Honey said as she discreetly slipped her .380 out of her purse. "I ain't playing with these motherfuckers."

"Yo, put the hammer away. I'll take care of it," Cam said as he noticed the three men getting closer and closer.

"No I'm not going to let nobody hurt you!" Honey spat. No longer after she said that her and Cam saw one of the men reach down into his waist as if he was trying to pull something out.

Honey wrapped her finger around the trigger and prepared to shoot. *"If this motherfucker take one more step I'mma clap him,"* she said to herself. Just as Honey got ready to pull the trigger, Cam put a calm hand over hers.

"Chill out baby," Cam whispered. He looked out into the crowd and saw the hard faced man who was reaching in his waistband throw a bottle up into the VIP section.

The bottle came nowhere close to hitting Cam or Honey, but that wasn't the point. Cam watched as his security snatched the bottle thrower from out of the crowd and beat him half to death.

"We already got paid so we can leave if you want." Cam turned and faced Honey. "I don't need you out here in harm's way." He didn't want to risk Honey's safety or put her in a harmful situation. There was too much money riding on the line to have her caught up in some bullshit.

"No fuck that! We ain't going nowhere," Honey declared. "We ain't running from nobody." As if right on cue, French Montana's song *"I Ain't Worried About Nothing"* came blaring through the speakers. Honey stood up on the couch and began to sing along. "Nigga I ain't worried bout nothing!"

The crowd went crazy when they saw Cam stand up on the couch and began to make it rain twenty dollar bills.

"Fuck it! If these niggaz wanna watch me, then I might as well give them something to look at, " Cam said to himself as he continued to enjoy himself. He noticed the dirty looks that Peanut and Red gave him, but he paid them no mind and continued to do him. As Cam stood on the couch making it rain, he felt his cell phone vibrate on his hip over a hundred times, but he didn't even bother to look down at the screen cause he knew the only person that would be

calling him back to back like that was Yolanda and right now he wasn't really in the mood to talk to her.

After dancing on the couch for five straight songs, Cam and Honey sat down and continued to get their drink on. Cam's face crumbled up when he saw Honey get ready to pour herself a drink in a fancy looking flute and then decided to drink straight from the bottle instead on some ratchet shit.

"Fuck is you doing?" Cam asked looking at Honey like she was crazy. He knew how ignorant, loud, and ratchet she could get when she was drunk and the last thing he needed was a drunken Honey.

"What?" Honey asked as if she didn't have a clue what Cam was talking about.

"Have some fucking class and drink out of a glass like a woman and not some hoe."

"I know you ain't talking to me like that," Honey huffed. "You must got me fucked up!"

"How many times I gotta tell you about your drinking?" Cam asked.

"I'm sorry daddy," Honey said draping her arm around Cam's neck. "I thought we was getting turnt up tonight?"

"What's with all this turnt up shit?" Cam questioned. He was from the old school and he wasn't up on the new school lingo.

"You know I love you to death right?" Honey said looking Cam in the eyes.

"I guess."

"Fuck you mean you guess? Cam stop playing with me," Honey yelled. When it came to her love for Cam, Honey didn't play no games. "I don't want you seeing Yolanda no more."

Cam sighed loudly. "Can we have a good night tonight please? I don't wanna talk about another woman right now. I'm with you so let's just enjoy the night."

Honey shook her head with a jealous look on her face. "Sweet talking Cam... I bet you don't wanna talk about that, but I don't give a fuck."

Right then and there Cam could tell that Honey was now officially drunk and the site alone disgusted him.

"Now like I was saying," she continued. "I don't want you seeing Yolanda no more Cam and if I find out you still creeping around with that raggedy bitch, it's gonna be some problems."

"I know," Cam said quickly.

"You patronizing me?"

Cam looked up and saw Peanut and Red headed in his direction. "Yo be on point," he said to Honey and then nodded towards the two men headed in their direction.

Honey took a swig from her bottle and then asked, "Ain't that your bum ass cousin?"

"I don't have a cousin no more," Cam said seriously.

Peanut and Red reached the entrance to the VIP section and were stopped by Honey's security.

"Fuck you think you going!?" Honey's head bodyguard, a man that went by the name Truck barked placing a solid strong paw on Peanuts chest.

"I need to holla at my cousin right quick," Peanut said and then went to side step the big man, but Truck swiftly eased to his left blocking Peanut's path.

"My man, check this out," Truck began. "Step the fuck off before I break your jaw."

Before things got out of hand, Cam wisely stepped in. "They cool. Let them through," he told Truck who looked like he was ready to put in some work on the two clowns that stood before him.

"You sure?" Truck asked never taking his eyes off the two men.

"Yeah they good," Cam said leading Peanut and Red over towards the sofas in the VIP section.

"Damn shorty looking like something," Red said openly undressing Honey with his eyes.

Honey sucked her teeth. "Nigga please!"

"So what's good?" Cam asked sitting down. He was ready to get down to business and see what the two men wanted.

Truck didn't like the vibe he was getting from the two men so he made sure he wasn't that far away from Honey.

"Listen," Peanut began. "I'mma cut straight to the chase. I'm willing to call the wolves off for a small fee," he said greedily rubbing his hands together.

"Extortion," Cam said. "You trying to extort me; your own cousin?"

"I wouldn't call it extortion. I like to call it more like looking out for family," Peanut smiled.

"Fuck outta here! We ain't with none of that!" Honey snapped. "We work too motherfucking hard to get where we are!"

"Bitch ain't nobody talking to you!" Peanut growled. "Stay out of a man's business and stay in a woman's place!"

"You super fly bum ass niggaz come over here talking all this fake tough fly shit like y'all built like that," Honey shot back. "I'm telling you now, y'all fucking with the wrong one cause I..."

Cam quickly cut Honey off. "Listen Peanut, I been trying to be nice to you cause you my cousin and all that, but now you violating so if you wanna take it to the streets all you gotta do is say so." Cam didn't want to get back on his old school street shit, but at the same time there was no way that he was going to let anyone extort him.

"I ain't got nothing to lose, but you on the other hand have a whole lot to lose so it's your call," Peanut said smiling. "Me and my niggaz are down for whatever and don't give a fuck about nothing or nobody!"

"Listen either you going to get in line or get lined up! What's it going to be!?" Red said from the sideline. He was tired of going back and forth with a coward like Cam.

"Listen B, I'mma tell you like this," Cam said in a serious stern tone. "Fuck y'all niggaz. See me in the streets."

"You sure that's what you wanna do?" Peanut asked. He was expecting Cam and Honey to fold and give in to his demands cause they didn't want no trouble, but he got a rude awakening.

Honey reached down in her bra, pulled out a wad of cash, and threw it in Peanut's face. The bills dramatically flew all over the place making things look worse than what they were.

As soon as the bills touched Peanut's face, he responded with a backhand across Honey's face that sent her flying out of her seat.

From there all hell broke loose. Cam jumped up and snuffed Peanut as the two went blow for blow right there in the VIP section in front of hundreds of party goers.

Red got ready to get in on the action, but a punch to the back of his head by Truck put his lights out before he even got a chance to swing.

Honey quickly shot to her feet and helped Cam as she threw several wild punches that landed on Peanut's face before the rest of her security came and tackled Peanut down to the floor. Once security had the situation under control Truck and two other security guards escorted Cam and Honey out a side door while the rest of their security took Peanut and Red out the back door and beat them half to death.

"YOU CAN'T BE SERIOUS"

Yolanda sat on the toilet looking at the positive pregnancy test that rested in her hand as tears streamed down her face. She loved Cam to death, but she wasn't sure if having his baby was a good idea at the moment. The other night she received a phone call from Cam and heard him and another woman having sex. He must have sat on his phone and dialed her number by accident. To have to hear Cam fucking another woman crushed Yolanda on the inside and had her feeling like shit.

Yolanda hopped up off the toilet and exited the bathroom when she heard her front door open. She stepped out the bathroom and saw Cam walking through the front door and from a first look she could tell that he had been drinking.

"What's up?" Cam asked as if he had somewhere else better to be.

"Why haven't I seen you in two weeks?" Yolanda asked with a slight attitude. She missed Cam and she was ready for him to come back home.

"Been busy."

"Been so busy that you couldn't call me?" Yolanda pressed. "But you can call me by mistake and let me hear you fucking another bitch though right?"

Cam sighed loudly. "That's what you called me over here for?"

"Fuck you Cam!" Yolanda snapped. "You can make time for everything and everybody, but me right? The only person that was there by your side from day one... You a trifling motherfucker!"

Cam stood to his feet and headed for the door. "Yo listen, don't call me no more. I'm tired of you and your bullshit," he said as if Yolanda was the one doing him wrong.

"Cam I'm pregnant," Yolanda blurted out. Her words seemed to stop Cam dead in his tracks.

"What you just said?"

"I said I'm pregnant," Yolanda repeated.

"By who?" Cam asked. Yeah it was a low blow, but at the moment he didn't care.

"Fuck you mean by who?" Yolanda barked. "Cam don't play yourself! You know I haven't been with nobody but you."

"How I know that?" Cam asked. "I don't know what you been out here doing; probably out here giving that pussy away like free lunch."

Yolanda was mad enough to rip Cam's head off of his shoulders. How could he speak to her like she wasn't shit after all they had been through?

"So that's what you think of me?" Yolanda asked trying to hold back her tears that were threatening to fall at any second.

"So what you going to do about that?" Cam asked eyeing Yolanda's stomach.

"What are you asking me?"

"You need to get rid of that shit," Cam told her coldly. "I ain't ready for no kids and neither are you!"

"Huh?" Yolanda sobbed. She couldn't believe that Cam was acting so heartless and talking to her like she was just some random chick instead of his high school sweet heart. "I think you should leave."

"I'll give you fifteen thousand if you get an abortion," Cam said pulling a huge wad of cash from his pocket.

Yolanda walked up and slapped the shit out of Cam. "Get the fuck out my house right now, you bastard!" she barked as she forcefully shoved him out the front door and then slammed it and locked it. She placed her back to the door and slid down to the floor and cried like a baby.

***

After Yolanda had told Cam about her being pregnant, he came up with a little plan on how to kill two birds with one stone.

Cam sat on the plush bed in a five star hotel and watched as Blondie did a seductive dance for him with some sexy fishnet stocking on and some shiny tall black hooker books. After the last time he saw Blondie, Cam planned on never seeing her again, but today was different. Today he needed Blondie. She just didn't know it yet.

"Yeah that's right. Shake that shit," Cam coached from the bed. He may not have really cared for Blondie, but he had to admit that she was as sexy as they came. Not to mention, she could move her body better than most strippers.

"You like that?" Blondie asked in a sexy husky voice as she made her ass jiggle like it had a mind of its own.

Cam gulped down the last of his drink and then pulled Blondie onto the bed with him. He whispered in her ear, "Come ride this dick."

"That's what you want? Huh?" Blondie growled as she planted her heeled feet down on the bed, squatted over Cam, reached back, and slipped his dick inside of her.

"Damnnnn," Blondie hissed as she sucked in air as she eased down on Cam's dick nice and slow. She loved how Cam's dick filled her up. It was a perfect fit.

Cam pulled Blondie's hair as she rode him, looked at her as she moaned, and stared into the haunting eyes of a woman who just wanted to be loved.

Blondie moved up and down, going up easy, and coming down hard. She did that over and over and over again. Cam held on to her while he watched her move, roll, and gyrate on top of him. She gripped the top of the headboard for support and leverage. Blondie bounced up and down on Cam's dick as if she was trying to break it, while loud moans escaped from her lips.

"You love this dick?" Cam asked as he slapped Blondie's ass.

"Ewww, I looooove this dick," Blondie growled like an animal.

"I'm bout to cum all over this dick!" she screamed as she bounced up and down even harder. "Argh, argh, argh... Shit!" Blondie moaned and cursed and held on to whatever she could hold on to. Her orgasm came hard and fast in a series of waves.

"Oooooh shit! Fuck!" Blondie cursed, panted, and jerked as her body began to quiver and shake. Cam fucked Blondie like she had never been fucked before and Blondie was loving every minute of it.

Cam sat up and placed his back against the head board and moved with Blondie. He could tell that she was ready to tap out, but he was just getting started. Cam thrust in and out of her with force. His thrust were brutal and unkind, but Blondie came down on top of him with equal or greater force each time clenching her teeth, growling, and challenging Cam, telling him to give her all he had.

Blondie's moans deepened as her nails dug deeper into Cam's skin as another orgasm took over her body. She held on to Cam until she stopped thrusting. She held him until she stopped coming.

"Oh my God!" Blondie huffed as she hopped off of Cam's dick. "I can't take no more!"

"But I ain't done yet," Cam said with a wicked smile on his face as he stroked himself in front of Blondie.

Immediately Blondie took as much of Cam as she could in her mouth and let out a light gag as she felt the head of his dick tickle the back of her throat.

Cam positioned Blondie directly in front of him on her knees as he stood straight up on the bed. Something about Blondie's fishnets and hooker boots turned Cam into an animal. He used both hands and gripped the sides of Blondie's head and went to town on her mouth. He fucked her mouth like he was trying to choke her. The more Blondie gagged, the further Cam went, until finally Blondie jerked her head back and let out a few coughs. She looked up at Cam with watery eyes and a smirk on her face, then went right back to trying to suck the skin off of Cam's dick.

Blondie made wet sounds with her mouth while her head moved 100 mph like she was possessed. Her mouth was wet and her determination was loud. Cam stroked Blondie's mouth a few more times before he pulled out and masturbated leaving his fluids all over Blondie's face and mouth.

Once Cam's work was finished, he pulled out his iPhone and snapped a picture of Blondie with her face covered in semen. "Yeah I think I'mma post this on Instagram later," he said with a devilish smirk on his face.

"You better not," was all Blondie said as she disappeared in the bathroom to clean herself up. While she was in the bathroom, Cam's mind went back to the last time he had saw Yolanda and she told him that she was pregnant. Her being pregnant and not wanting to get rid of the baby was beginning to piss him off.

When Blondie returned from the bathroom she noticed Cam had a serious look on his face as if something was bothering him. "What's wrong?"

"You should be asking what ain't wrong," Cam said helping himself to another drink. He knew he could manipulate Blondie and make her do anything he wanted. He just had to make her feel like he needed and really loved her.

"Anything I can do to help?" Blondie asked as she plopped down onto the bed next to Cam. Blondie had a bit of a gut, but her small waist and curvaceous hips drew attention away from it.

Cam eyed Blondie's ass and admired its jiggle as she sat down. "I got a little problem," he began. "I don't really want to involve you, but I don't know who else to go to," he said laying it on thick.

"What is it baby? You know I'll do anything for you," Blondie said sincerely meaning every last word she spoke.

"It's Yolanda," Cam sighed. "She's pregnant; that's why when she popped up at the hotel I got you up off of her and didn't let you whip her ass," he lied. "I'm not ready for no kids."

"You out building your brand and career; a child ain't going to do nothing but slow you down right now," Blondie said as she helped herself to a strong drink. "That bitch Yolanda is bugging right now," she spat. The reason she was salty was because if anyone was going to have Cam's child, it was going to be her. "So what you need me to do?"

Just the words Cam wanted to hear. "I was thinking maybe you and a few of your home girls could maybe run down on her and rough her up a bit. Don't kill her, but rough her up so she can't have the baby."

"Done," Blondie said quickly not even giving it a second thought. This idea was just what Blondie needed. First she would get rid of Yolanda and get her out of the picture and then once that was done, her next objective would be Honey. Everything was going according to plan and soon she would be Cam's only girl.

"Yo, I'mma be out of town for a few weeks with Honey. I'd prefer you take care of that while I'm away," Cam suggested.

"No problem baby. I'll take care of it. Anything for you," Blondie smiled devilishly.

"SECURITY"

E ver since the beef with Cam and Peanut began, Cam had beefed up his security team and Honey hated it. She hated having to be watched everywhere she went. There were certain times when she just wanted to be left alone.

"How much longer do we have to roll around with all this security?" Honey asked with an attitude.

"Until I say so," Cam replied. Honey had been in an ugly mood for the past two days because Cam refused to let her buy her money hungry mother a new Benz. It seemed like the only time Honey's mother called her was to beg for money and Cam refused to sit back and let anybody take advantage of Honey. Not to mention, Yolanda being pregnant was still fresh on his mind.

"So I can't buy my mother a car, but we can spend unnecessary money on this security bullshit?" Honey snapped. "I don't tell you what to do with your money so..."

"Bitch you not buying your moms a car and that's that," Cam barked cutting Honey off. He was sick and tired of going back and forth with her about nonsense.

"Fuck you!" Honey growled as she attempted to get up off the bed and storm out the bedroom, but Cam grabbed her wrist in a firm grip.

"Bitch what I told you about your mouth!?" he growled as he forcefully sat Honey back down on the bed and began to unfasten his pants.

"Stop Cam; get off me," Honey protested as she struggled to jerk free from Cam's grip.

Cam pulled his dick out from his boxers and jammed it in Honey's mouth. "What I told you about that mouth of yours!? Huh?" Cam barked as he fucked Honey's mouth with a ferocious force. Honey gagged, coughed, and choked on Cam's length as she did her best to take Cam's entire length down her throat.

"That's it! Take it bitch!" Cam gasped, thrusting his pelvis harder and faster into Honey's mouth.

Honey moaned loudly as she popped Cam's dick out of her mouth and turned her attention to Cam's balls holding them in her hand and licking them assiduously like a cat. After a few licks, Cam jammed his dick back into Honey mouth and stroked it like his life depended on it. Saliva leaked from the corners of Honey's mouth and began to roll down her chin down onto her chest.

Cam's legs buckled slightly and then suddenly he pulled out and shot his load spraying cum all over Honey's face.

Honey quickly pushed Cam up off of her and sucked her teeth. "You better not had gotten none in my hair," she huffed and then disappeared into the bathroom.

Cam laid on the bed in deep thought. In the past month his life had been spiraling out of control. He had just gotten a call from his lawyer the other day telling him that his father was planning on suing him for the fight they had outside over at his mother's house. Also he had been hearing rumors in the streets that Peanut and Red were out riding around in search of him, and on top of that Yolanda was no longer answering his calls. Just as Cam thought his night couldn't get any worse, Honey stepped out of the bathroom with a mini skirt on, some heels, and a face full of makeup.

"Fuck you going?"

"Out," Honey snapped. It was obvious that she was still upset about not being able to buy her mother a car. If she would have been able to beat Cam up, she would have.

"Yo stop playing with me," Cam barked. "I said where the fuck you going?"

"I'm going out to have a drink," Honey sucked her teeth. "And no I'm not taking no security with me either!"

Cam quickly jumped up off the bed and made his way over to where Honey stood.

"I'm telling you right now Cam, don't put your hands on me cause we'll be up in this bitch fighting tonight," she warned.

Cam leaned over and kissed her on the cheek. "You wanna go out, fine. Go have a good time and your security is going with you."

"I'm not a baby. I know how to walk around by myself."

"You can't do those types of things anymore. You are a celebrity now. You can no longer do the simple small things that you used to do. You just can't," Cam tried explaining.

"Well I'm still not going out with all that stupid ass security! This shit don't make no sense!" she said while she folded her arms across her chest.

"Okay you don't have to go out with a shit load of security, but you're not leaving out this house without Truck by your side and that's final," Cam told her.

"I can live with that," Honey smiled and gave Cam a kiss on the lips. "This place is a mess. First thing tomorrow morning I'm hiring us a maid."

"Have a good time and remember, you are a celebrity now, which means all eyes are always going to be on you," Cam told her as he escorted her downstairs. Immediately he spotted Truck.

"Listen I'mma need you to keep a close eye on her tonight," Cam said in a hushed tone. "And don't let her drink too much."

"You got it boss," Truck said and like that him and Honey was out the door.

As soon as Honey stepped foot out the door, Cam's mind immediately began to think of which one of his side chicks he would give the pleasure of spending time with him tonight. He knew it was wrong, but at the moment it felt like the right thing to do according to him.

***

After driving around for damn near an hour Honey finally decided to spend her night hanging out in a low key type of lounge. The place was a hole in the wall type of joint, but Honey didn't mind. Tonight she didn't really feel like being in the spotlight so the lounge was perfect. She just hated the fact that now she could never go anywhere without a team of security guards.

"You sure this where you wanna hang out tonight?" Truck asked as he pulled the Escalade alongside the curb.

"Yeah, I don't really feel like being in the spotlight tonight, you know?"

"I can dig it," was all Truck said.

Out of all her security guards, Honey liked Truck the most. He was a cool guy and he went above and beyond to protect her and keep her safe.

Truck led the way inside the lounge making sure things were safe. The place looked way better on the inside than it did on the outside.

Truck went to speak to one of the promoters about a VIP section when Honey tapped him on the shoulder and dismissed that idea.

"That won't be necessary. The bar will be fine," Honey said and then headed for the bar. Tonight she didn't want to be treated like a celebrity. Tonight she wanted to be treated like a regular normal person.

Honey took a seat on the barstool and ordered a bottle of champagne. The place wasn't empty, but it wasn't packed either. The bartender handed Honey a bottle along with a wine glass.

"Nah I'm good. You can keep the glass," Honey said and turned the bottle up to her lips and began to guzzle straight from the bottle on some ratchet shit. She knew if Cam was there, she wouldn't have had been doing that, but at the moment she could care less about Cam. She loved Cam to death, but he was really starting to get on her nerves.

It took about only five minutes before a fan recognized Honey and began crying and screaming drawing attention over towards the bar area. Thirty minutes later, the lounge was packed to its capacity with people yelling and screaming to take a picture and get an autograph from Honey.

At first Truck suggested that they be escorted out the back door, but Honey refused. She hated being a celebrity, but at the end of the day she loved all of her fans so instead of enjoying her night, she decided to take pictures with each and every fan and sign as many autographs as she could. What started out as going out just to get away from the house for a minute, turned into a major event.

"It's was nice meeting you," Honey said to a lovely couple. Just as she was getting ready to leave, a woman with a nice shape and a head full of blonde weave approached her. "How you doing? You lucky, you caught me. I was just about to leave," Honey smiled. "What can I do for you today, a picture, an autograph, or both?"

"What you can do is stay the fuck away from my man," Blondie said in a matter of fact tone. She didn't like Honey because she was her biggest competition, so her plan was to try and cause a rift between her and Cam.

"I'm sorry, what was that?" Honey asked just to be sure she wasn't hearing things.

"You heard me hoe," Blondie snapped. "I know you and my man work together and all that, but keep it strictly business bitch or else I'mma come see you and that's word to everything I love."

Honey let out a slight laugh. "You popcorn hoes kill me," she shook her head. "First of all there's no way that Cam would ever take a bitch like you serious, that's number one and number two, why would he want that when he got all of this at home?" Honey asked striking a pose.

Blondie got ready to come back and say some fly shit, but before she got a chance, Honey took a swig from her bottle and spit a mouthful of champagne in Blondie's face and then followed up with a quick right hook. Before Blondie got a chance to react, Truck quickly stepped in and shoved Blondie down to the floor.

Honey was then quickly escorted out the back exit of the club and rushed into the backseat of the Escalade.

Before the Escalade pulled off, Blondie came flying out the back door and began to beat and bang on the back window until finally Truck pulled off.

"Who the fuck was that crazy bitch?" Truck asked peeking at Honey through the rearview mirror.

"Some nobody," Honey brushed it off, but on the inside she was furious and she couldn't wait to get home so she could confront Cam. She was sick and tired of him and his bullshit. It seemed like once Honey got rid of one chick, two more would pop up to take that one's place and honestly it was beginning to be too much.

When the Escalade pulled up to the mansion, Honey immediately spotted an unfamiliar car parked in the driveway. "Who car is that?"

"I don't know," Truck replied as he pulled up right behind the car and let the engine die.

"NEW MOUTH"

C am sat on the couch watching the head of some light skin chick he'd just met a few weeks ago bob up and down between his legs. The woman skillfully licked up and down the shaft of Cam's dick making sure not to miss a spot. Her tongue slowly made its way back up to the head. She looked up at Cam for a second and then spit on his dick, the whole time never taking her eyes off of him. "You like that don't you?"

Cam was about to say some slick, nasty, porn star type of shit back to the chick until he heard the sound of the front door opening and then slamming shut. "Oh shit!" He quickly pushed the woman's head from in between his legs and began fixing his pants as the sound of Honey's heels stabbing the floor grew louder and louder.

Honey came around the corner and saw Cam and some woman sitting on the couch with suspicious looks on their faces. "What's up?" she asked Cam, but her eyes were stuck on the chick that sat next to him.

"Oh hey baby wassup?" Cam stuttered. "What you doing here? I thought you were going out?"

"Who is this bitch and what the fuck is she doing in our house?" Honey asked ignoring Cam's question.

"Listen," Cam said trying to buy himself a little time so he could come up with a lie that was believable. "You told me we needed a maid so I was trying to surprise you, but..."

"Nigga please!" Honey snapped as she smoothly slipped out of her four inch heels and removed her earrings from her ear. "What the fuck is this bitch doing in my house!?" she said to Cam and then lunged toward the woman who sat on the couch with a cute little smirk on her face. Before Cam got a chance to hold Honey back, the girl who sat next to him on the couch was already on the floor getting pounded on.

"Yo chill… You wilding right now!" Cam barked as he roughly removed Honey from up off of the girl. "Chill the fuck out before you get sued behind this shit!"

"I don't give a fuck about that!" Honey yelled as she pushed off of Cam and ran to the kitchen and grabbed a sharp knife and pointed it at Cam.

"Yo, put that knife down and stop acting stupid before somebody gets hurt," Cam said with a straight face, but on the inside he was nervous.

"No fuck that!" Honey countered as she ran after the girl and chased her all throughout the house with the knife until finally Truck and Cam tackled her down to the floor and removed the knife from her hands.

"I got her. Go get shorty out the crib," Cam said holding Honey down while Truck went and escorted Cam's lady friend off the premises.

Once Truck and the woman were gone, Cam let Honey up off the floor. "Yo, you gotta chill. You be bugging..." Before Cam could even finish his sentence, Honey had stole on him. The punch caught Cam off guard and before he knew it, his shirt was ripped and Honey was swinging wildly throwing punches from all angles. "What the fuck is wrong with you!?" Cam yelled when he finally was able to restrain Honey.

"The girl with the Blonde hair!" Honey screamed. "You fucked her, didn't you? Didn't you?"

"Blonde hair...girl...like what is you talking about?" Cam asked faking ignorance. "I'm not fucking nobody but you," he lied. "Where's all this crazy shit coming from?"

"The girl told me that you and her are fucking!"

"What girl?"

"The girl with the blonde hair!" Honey said taking one last swing at Cam, but this time his reflexes were on point and he easily blocked the blow.

"You bugging right now. You need to chill."

"Fuck you Cam!" Honey spat. "I'm not bugging! You bugging! You gonna miss me when I'm gone!"

"You right," Cam said in a sarcastic manner. Every woman he had been with all told him the same thing and every time it was the farthest from the truth.

"You don't like it when I'm nice. You like to make me act like a damn fool, don't you?" Honey barked as she walked up on Cam.

"Chill," Cam said as he quickly grabbed Honey's wrist so she couldn't hit him. He knew he was dead wrong, but for some reason he just never could admit when he was in the wrong.

"You're gonna miss me when I'm gone," Honey sobbed as she went upstairs to the bedroom leaving Cam standing there looking stupid.

***

Cam sat over in the bar area with Truck as the two men sipped on some Vodka and orange juice. Things in Cam's life were really out of control and the sad thing was, he knew how to stop it, he just chose not to. In Cam's mind he didn't see the harm in a having *"a few"* women. He was raised on the motto, more is always better.

"So what you going to do about this situation?" Truck asked as he leaned back comfortably in his chair.

"I don't know," Cam shook his head. "It just seems like everything has been fucking up lately." He paused to take a sip from his drink. "It's like no matter what I do, somebody is gonna end up mad or getting hurt."

"You can't play with a woman's heart," Truck told him. "I've seen a lot of brothers fuck themselves in the end by trying to have their cake and eat it too," Truck pointed out. "The ending is always ugly."

"So what am I supposed to do, just be with one woman?" Cam asked looking at Truck like he was insane.

"Listen Cam, you have a lot going for yourself right now. A lot of women see you as a meal ticket," Truck explained. "And every one of them bitches wants to be Honey. All these women try to dress like her, act like her, and some even try to look like her," he pointed out. "All I'm saying is upstairs in that bedroom; you have a *"good woman"*, a woman that would give her own life to save yours. Don't fuck it up!"

Just as those words left Trucks lips, the two men heard the doorbell ring.

"Expecting company?" Truck asked looking over at Cam. He shook his head no as he watched Truck make his way over to the door. Seconds later Cam saw Yolanda step through the front door with a hurt and sad look on her face. He could tell that she had been stressing herself out since the last time the two had spoken.

"Fuck you want?" Cam said in a cold nasty tone. He figured since Yolanda had dropped by she was there to meet his demands.

"We need to talk," Yolanda said making her way towards the bar.

"I'm listening," Cam sipped from his drink. On the outside he was acting cold, but on the inside it felt good to see Yolanda again and to be honest he kind of missed her. Of course he would never tell her that though.

"We need to talk about this baby that's in my stomach," Yolanda said.

"Boss if you need me, I'm going to be over here," Truck said as he dismissed himself not wanting to hear anymore or be involved in Cam's mess.

"What do we have to talk about and why are you here? You know Honey don't like you."

"Fuck Honey! I'm here to talk to you about a serious matter," Yolanda huffed. "Me and you not speaking to one another is not helping the situation."

"And you keeping the baby is?" Cam shot back. "Having a baby ain't gonna keep no man," he said taking a shot. He knew just how to piss Yolanda off and that was his objective.

"I'm not having this baby to keep you," Yolanda corrected him. "I can raise this baby all on my own, but that's not what I want to do. I want my child to know his father and I want my child to know that his father loves him or her."

"Fuck that!" Cam snapped. "You trying to have that baby so you can take all my money."

Immediately Yolanda knew that was the alcohol talking and not Cam. The Cam she knew and fell in love with would never speak to her in this manner. "Who are you and what's gotten into you?"

"Man listen, me and you ain't together no more so I don't see the point in you having this baby, point blank, period. Besides, how I even know its mines?" he said. It was a low blow, but at the moment Cam didn't care.

"How you know what's yours?" Honey asked descending the stairs. She held a wine glass in her hand and a silk Chinese robe covered her naked body. It was as if she appeared out of nowhere and immediately Cam knew shit was about to get ugly. Honey's manicured toes came down one step at a time until she was downstairs at the bar area along with Cam and Yolanda.

"How do you know what's yours?" Honey asked looking directly at Cam. She was still pissed off from earlier and she was looking for any reason to act a fool.

"Go back upstairs baby," Cam said in a smooth tone. "Yolanda was just leaving."

"What the fuck is this bitch doing here and why the fuck is she in my house!?" Honey asked raising her voice. She was drunk and didn't give a fuck about nothing no more.

"I'm here because I'm pregnant," Yolanda said spilling the beans.

"By who?" Honey asked with a raised brow. "Pregnant by who?"

Before things got out of hand, Truck stepped in between Honey and Cam.

"You still out here fucking this raggedy ass bitch!?" Honey snapped taking a step forward, but Truck stopped her progress. "You see, you gonna make me kill one of these nondescript bitches!"

"Why don't you calm the fuck down?!" Yolanda said. "This ain't got nothing to do with you!"

Honey tossed her drink in Yolanda's face. "I'm tired ya mouth hoe!"

Truck quickly had to scramble over to Yolanda and keep the two women separated. While Truck held Yolanda back, Honey snuck in a cheap shot and stole on Cam and tried to scratch his eyes out. In the heat of the battle, Cam slammed Honey down to the floor and restrained her.

"Yo chill the fuck out!" Cam yelled as he forcefully yanked Honey up to her feet and roughly escorted her up the stairs.

As Yolanda and Truck stood downstairs they heard loud noises coming from upstairs, noises that sounded like furniture was being moved, ugly curse words filled the air, and then seconds later Cam returned downstairs with a few scratches on his face and neck.

"You alright?" Yolanda asked. Her and Cam might not have been on good terms at the moment, but she still had a soft spot for him in her heart.

"I'm good."

"You got some alcohol or peroxide here?"

"I said I'm good," Cam huffed as he ran his hand over his head. "Listen, I think it would be best for the both of us if you got rid of the baby. All it's going to do is continue to cause problems."

"Problems for who?" Yolanda folded her arms across her chest. "I know you ain't talking about that bitch upstairs."

Cam said nothing, but the look on his face said it all.

"You a real scum bag," Yolanda said as tears rolled down her cheeks. "Fuck you! I'm having my baby and if you don't want to be a part of me and this baby's life, then that's your loss," she said and then stormed off.

"Yolanda wait," Cam called out. "Please don't do this."

"Fuck you!" was all Yolanda said and just like that she was gone.

"Looks like you done gone and got yourself caught up in the middle of some shit, some serious shit at that," Truck pointed out.

"Yeah I know."

"So how do you plan on getting yourself out of this one?"

"I have no idea," Cam said with a defeated look on his face.

Seconds later Honey came storming down the steps with a duffle bag in her hand and an attitude on her face.

"Where you going?" Cam asked.

"I ain't fucking with you no more," was Honey's response. "You still wanna play these childish games and I'm too old for that bullshit."

"So that's what you do? When shit get a little rough, you break out on a nigga?"

"I ain't breaking out nothing. If you were to treat me the way I treat..."

"Just get the fuck out!" Cam said rudely cutting Honey off. If she wanted to leave, he wasn't about to beg her to stay. "You ain't doing shit but slowing me down anyway," he said with a flick of his wrist in a dismissive manner.

"You ain't shit! I hate you!" Honey spat and then walked out the front door.

"I better go with her to make sure she's okay and doesn't do anything stupid," Truck said.

"Fuck that bitch!" Cam slurred. He was tired of all the bullshit. If Honey didn't want to be with him no more than so be it. She would now be another man's problem.

"I'mma go make sure she's alright," Truck said as he went after Honey.

"I'M SORRY"

When Yolanda pulled up in front of her house she spotted an unfamiliar car parked by her driveway. She couldn't see who was inside, but from where she sat it looked to be a man's silhouette. When she pulled into the driveway she noticed both the driver and passenger door of the mystery car open and out hopped two men. At first Yolanda was nervous, that was until she recognized the two men as Peanut and Red.

"Well look what we have here," Red said in a slurred tone as he undressed Yolanda with his eyes.

Yolanda rolled her eyes and then looked at Peanut. "What do you two fools want?"

"Just here looking for Cam," Peanut said in a neutral tone. "Why don't you go inside and tell him to come out here?"

From the two men's body language, Yolanda could tell that they were strapped and probably planned on doing harm to Cam. Her and Cam might have been beefing at the moment, but he was still the father of her unborn child and she didn't want to see anything bad happen to him. "He ain't here."

"Then where is he?" Peanut asked with a raised brow.

Yolanda said, "I don't know. I don't fuck with him no more."

"Word?" Peanut said with a disbelieving look on his face. "Listen, stop playing and tell us where this nigga Cam is at."

"I just told you, I don't..."

Before Yolanda could finish her sentence, Peanut backed out a chrome .45 and put it to her head. Right on cue Red snatched Yolanda's two thousand dollar bag out of her hand, removed the house keys, and let himself inside her home.

Peanut roughly shoved Yolanda through the front door and tossed her down to the floor.

"Peanut why are you doing this?" Yolanda cried. "Cam is your cousin," she pointed out hoping that, that would make him rethink the foul act that he was getting ready to commit.

"That nigga ain't my cousin," Peanut said with his face crumbled up. "That nigga is a sellout."

Peanut was jealous of Cam's success and he hated him for not giving him a free handout and letting him ride his wave for free. In Peanut's mind, he felt that Cam took better care of his women than he did his own family.

"Peanut please don't do this. I'm pregnant," Yolanda pleaded.

"Now niggaz is pregnant." Peanut shook his head with a disgusted look on his face. "I thought you just told me that you don't fuck with Cam no more?"

After searching the entire house to make sure they were alone Red returned and handcuffed Yolanda's hands behind her back.

"Where the bread at?" Red asked with a hungry look in his eyes.

"Tell us where the money is and I won't hurt you," Peanut said. "Please don't make me do something that I don't want to do."

Yolanda could tell that if she didn't tell Peanut where Cam's stash was, that he would make good on his threats.

"There's a safe in our bedroom, in the back of the walk in closet. The combination is 55,4,15," Yolanda told him. She watched as Red ran upstairs towards their bedroom.

"You used to be cool," Yolanda said looking up at Peanut. "What happened to you?"

"You know what they say... Niggaz is cool until they ain't cool," Peanut smirked. "It didn't have to be like this. All Cam had to do was look out for his family."

"You're a grown ass man! Why would you even want another man to have to take care of you?" Yolanda spat. She then received a kick to the face from Peanut for her disrespect.

Minutes later Red returned with a half full pillowcase in his hand. "Jackpot," he said with a smile smeared across his face.

Before Peanut had to chance to reply, the front door came busting open catching everyone off guard. In charged a man wearing all black with a black ski mask covering his face and a gun in his hand followed by a second gunman.

Yolanda watched in horror as the gunman blew Peanut's head off right in front of her sending blood and brain fragments splashing across her face. The gunman then turned his attention to Red who stood frozen like a deer caught in the headlights. The first bullet exploded in his chest while the second one placed a gaping hole in his throat.

The gunman then turned his focus on Yolanda.

"Please don't do this," Yolanda pleaded with tears running down her face.

The gunman fired off two more shot and then he was out the door. The two bullets exploded in Yolanda's chest with extreme force leaving her lying on the floor to die in a pool of her own blood.

***

Cam laid sleep on the couch when he was awakened by a loud knock at his door. Cam jumped up and the first thing he thought was it had to be the cops at his door. He opened the door and on the other side stood one of Yolanda's friends, a skinny chick by the name of Rose. Cam and Rose never really seen eye to eye due to the fact of Cam and all of his other women. Rose always went out of her way to tell Yolanda some foul shit about him.

"Fuck you doing here?" Cam asked giving Rose an ugly look.

"Yolanda has just been shot!" Rose said in a panicked tone of voice. "We have to get to the hospital!"

"What happened? Slow down... Shot, who got shot?"

"Yolanda!"

"Bullshit! "Cam said in disbelief. "She just left here no longer than an hour ago."

"Fuck all that! We need to get to the hospital!" Rose said with urgency.

Cam threw on a pair of jeans, a white tee, and was out the door in a flash. Him and Rose hopped in his Benz and made a beeline straight to the hospital.

"Who in their right mind would want to shoot Yolanda?" Rose said out loud. "Does she have any enemies?"

"No everyone loves Yolanda. You know that," Cam said keeping his eyes on the road.

"Mmm...hmmm," Rose huffed giving Cam the evil eye. "Probably one of your crazy ass bitches, who shot her."

All Cam could do was shake his head. He thought about replying, but decided against it. At the moment he didn't feel like going back and forth with a man basher like Rose.

"You ain't gonna learn about playing with a woman's heart until one of these women fuck around and kills you," Rose said. "People like you don't get it until it's too late and that's sad."

"Do you have a man? No I didn't think so!" Cam said not even giving Rose a chance to respond. "It's always you chicks that ain't got no man trying to give relationship advice. If you were such an expert on relationships, then why are you single?"

"Cause I choose to be, that's why."

"Yeah I know," Cam said sarcastically.

"Can't no man do nothing for me that I can't do for myself," Rose capped back. "I have my own. I'm not one of those chicks that have to put up with a whole bunch of bullshit to keep a man. If a man is too stupid to not know my worth, then I'll just be by myself."

"You just jealous because Yolanda got a man and you don't," Cam said.

"Jealous?" Rose echoed with her face crumbled up. "Let me explain something to you," she said turning to face him. "First of all, Yolanda doesn't have a man, she has a little ass boy that thinks he's God's gift to women when in all actuality he's more of a curse than a gift. You don't even know what it is to be a real man, so don't speak that jealous shit to me."

Cam got a kick out of ruffling Rose's feathers. To him it was funny to see her get all worked up over nothing. "Like I said, you jealous cause if you wasn't you would be happy for Yolanda."

"Happy that she's in the hospital probably because one of them ratchet bitches you fuck with done shot her?" Rose shook her head. "Yeah I'm super jealous, matter fact don't say shit else to me. You're an ignorant classless fool!"

Cam pulled up to the hospital and stormed inside with Rose hot on his heels. He tried to enter Yolanda's room, but was stopped immediately by a detective.

"Sorry no one is allowed pass this point," the detective said placing a firm hand on Cam's chest.

"That's my girl. I have to make sure she's alright," Cam said.

"Sir the doctors are in there operating. No one is allowed back there at the moment," the detective told him.

"Is it bad?"

"Detective Washington," the detective said extending his hand to Cam.

Cam looked down at the detective's hand like it had just been removed from a toilet bowl and left him hanging. Hood rule #101, fuck the police.

"Did Yolanda have any enemies that would have wanted to hurt her?" Detective Washington asked as he removed a pen and small pad from his pocket.

"Yo check this out," Cam said in a frustrated tone. "My shorty is laid up in a fucking hospital bed. I'm not really in the mood to be answering no bullshit questions."

"With or without you, I'm going to get to the bottom of this," Detective Washington told him.

Right at that very moment, a light bulb went off in Cam's head. He quickly turned and exited the hospital leaving Rose and Detective Washington just standing there with a confused look on their faces. He hopped in his Benz and peeled out of the hospital parking lot like a mad man.

"BITCH YOU MUST BE CRAZY!"

B londie stood in her kitchen dressed in all black with a shot glass in her hand. She quickly threw back the Vodka and downed the liquid fire in one gulp. She knew what she was getting ready to do was wrong, but to earn Cam's love she was willing to do whatever it took.

"Get it together," she coached herself as she heard a loud strong knock at the door. Blondie walked over to the door, looked through the peep hole, and smiled.

"Heeeey baby," she sang in a happy tone as she opened the door and saw Cam standing on the other side.

"Bitch!" Cam growled as he wrapped his hands around Blondie's neck and forced her back inside of her apartment. Before Blondie got a chance to say a word, Cam had already slapped the taste out of her mouth.

"Cam stop please!" Blondie yelled as she did her best to cover her face and stop Cam from rearranging her face.

Cam got up and kicked Blondie in her ribs. "Bitch I told you to hurt Yolanda, not shoot her!" he yelled as he delivered another kick to her ribs.

"What are you talking about? I didn't shoot anyone!" Blondie yelled from down on the floor. She had a scared and nervous look on her face.

"Stop lying!" Cam yelled and faked like he was going to hit Blondie again causing her to flinch.

"I'm not lying! I swear to God!" Blondie yelled through a bloody mouth and a busted lip. "I was just getting ready to go handle that now," she pleaded.

"Yo Blondie I'm telling you right now, you better not be lying to me or else I'mma break your motherfucking face!" Cam threatened. "Did you shoot Yolanda?"

"No Cam I didn't shoot anybody," Blondie cried holding the side of her face. "I don't even have a gun!"

"Fuck!" Cam cursed out loud. For some strange reason he believed Blondie, but if she didn't shoot Yolanda, then who did?

Cam took one look at Blondie and immediately felt bad for putting his hands on her, but his anger had gotten the best of him. "I'm sorry baby," he said as he went and grabbed some ice for Blondie's face. "Here put this on your face."

Blondie accepted the ice and then asked, "What happened to Yolanda?"

"Somebody shot her," Cam said with a defeated look on his face.

"Is she...?" Blondie said not wanting to come straight out and ask.

"Nah she's not dead, but whoever did this is going to be," Cam said meaning every word he said. Yeah he may not have wanted Yolanda to have the baby, but at the same time he didn't want her dead either. The only other person he thought could or would do something like this was Honey. Ever since the blow up that he, Yolanda, and Honey had at the crib, Honey had been MIA.

Cam may not have known where Honey was at the moment, but what he did know was that she was throwing a big party for her birthday in two weeks; a party that he would definitely be at. He had questions and the only person who could answer them was Honey.

"Are you alright?" Blondie asked holding a Ziploc bag filled with ice up to the side of her face.

"Yeah I'm good. Sorry about your face," he said shamefully looking down at the floor.

"It's okay," Blondie tried to smile, but Cam could tell that it was hurting her face muscles.

Cam pulled a couple of bills from his pocket and sat them down on the counter as if that would make Blondie's pain go away. "I'mma holla at you later."

"Please call me tonight Cam," Blondie pleaded. "I would really like to hear your voice before the night is out," she said as tears began to fall from her eyes.

"Stop all that cry baby stuff, I promise I'm going to call you tonight. You got my word on that," Cam lied with a straight face.

"Okay, it don't matter how late it is. I'll be up," Blondie assured him and then hugged him like she was never going to see him again.

"Trust me I got you," Cam said and like that he was gone just as quick as he came.

"SURPRISE, SURPRISE"

Two days had passed since Yolanda had been shot and the police still had no clues or leads. Cam entered the hospital lobby with a dozen roses in his hands. He felt bad about what had happened to Yolanda and for some strange reason deep down inside his conscious was telling him that somehow it was his fault that she had been shot. He couldn't prove it, but that's what his gut was telling him.

Cam strolled through the hospital like he owned the place. As he walked by, several of the nurses who worked there gawked at him boosting up his already humongous ego. When Cam reached Yolanda's room, he stopped short when he heard loud laughter coming from inside the room. He quickly checked the room number at the side of the door just to make sure he was at the right room. Once he was sure that he was at the correct room, he entered.

Cam stepped foot in the room and the first thing he saw was Yolanda sitting up in the bed with a smile on her face. The next thing he noticed was a big brolic nigga sitting over in the cut. Cam quickly sized the man up in his head. The man had to weigh around 240 pounds and he looked to be all solid muscles. His bald head only made him look even more diesel. The next thing Cam noticed was the sleeve of tattoo's that covered both of the man's arms. Immediately Cam put two and two together, big muscles and a lot of tattoo's only meant one thing. The man sitting in Yolanda's hospital room must have just come home from prison.

"Fuck going on up in here?" Cam asked Yolanda, but his eyes were stuck on the brolic nigga sitting next to her bed.

"Hey Cam," Yolanda said as if everything was cool. "What you doing here?"

"Fuck you mean what am *I* doing here!" Cam snapped.

"Yo my man," the diesel nigga said standing to his feet. "You going to have to chill with all that cursing and keep your voice down, Yolanda has been through a lot these last couple of days," he said as if he had known Yolanda for years and that only pissed Cam off even further.

"Keep my voice down?" Cam echoed looking at the muscle man like he was crazy. "Nigga don't motherfucking tell me to keep nothing down. I'll talk as loud as I want and ain't nobody gonna shut me up! How bout that!"

"Listen I asked you nicely the first time. Next I'mma let my hands do all the talking," the muscle man threatened and from the look on his face everyone in the room could tell that he wasn't bullshitting.

"Richard it's not that serious," Yolanda said trying to calm the diesel man down a bit. As soon as she saw Cam step foot in the room, she knew it was sure to be a problem.

"Who the fuck is this clown?" Cam asked with venom dripping from his voice.

"This is Richard. He's an old friend of mine," Yolanda told him. "He heard about my accident on Facebook and he just came to make sure I was alright."

"So now you fucking niggaz from Facebook?"

"First of all I'm not fucking anybody, that's number one and number two, whoever I choose to fuck is my business. Me and you aren't together anymore!" Yolanda yelled. "I lost the baby so you got your wish. Now you can go be happy with your bitches!"

* * *

The fact that another man could potentially be a part of Yolanda's life didn't sit well with Cam. Even though Cam didn't want Yolanda anymore, he didn't want anyone else to have her either, especially not the big diesel man who was sitting in her room at the moment.

"I knew you was a hoe," Cam said with a disgusted look on his face. "I should have left you right on the streets where I found you," he said as he cleared his throat and hog spit in Yolanda's face.

Once Cam spit in Yolanda's face, Richard shot to his feet and charged at Cam. Cam quickly took the dozen roses and swung them like it was a baseball bat.

Richard raised one of his massive arms blocking the roses from hitting him in the face and grabbed Cam by his throat with his other hand.

Cam was able to land a quick two piece to the big man's jaw before the hospital's security stormed inside the room and separated the two men stopping them from killing each other.

"I'mma clap you the next time I see you!" Cam yelled as security ushered him out of Yolanda's room. Out in the hallway Cam fought and struggled with security to get back at the diesel man in Yolanda's room until finally Detective Washington stepped in and escorted Cam out of the hospital.

"Calm down and talk to me," Detective Washington said once the two were outside. "What seems to be the problem?"

"Ain't no problem," Cam snapped and then spun off leaving the detective right where he stood.

"THE NIGHT LIFE"

Honey sat over in the VIP section of the club doing her best to enjoy her birthday, but just because she had a smile on her face didn't mean that she was happy. It had been over two weeks since the last time she had seen or heard from Cam and to be honest it was killing her to be away from the man that she loved and felt like she couldn't live without. But at the end of the day she had to show Cam that she would leave him if his bullshit didn't stop. She had to let him know that she wasn't just going to sit back and let him walk all over her.

Truck stood close to Honey making sure she was safe and well protected along with several other bodyguards that Cam had hired to keep Honey safe. As Honey sat getting her sip on, the entire vibe of the party changed when she spotted Cam stroll up in the club with two model looking women draped on each of his arms.

"You see this the shit I be talking about," Honey said to herself as she sized the two chicks up in her head. Instantly visions of Cam fucking both of the women at the same time filled Honey's brain.

Cam stepped in the club looking like a million bucks. Two iced out chains hung from his neck and bounced off his chest with every step he took. On his wrist was an iced out watch that he couldn't even pronounce the name of, but it was expensive and it looked nice. The two chicks that attended the club with him looked flawless, and the huge asses that they paid for turned the head of every man in the club.

Several men greeted Cam and gave him props, complimenting him on his taste of women. Cam knew Honey was in the building and more than likely watching him so he purposely posted up over by the bar and continued to mingle with other party goers paying her no mind.

Just like he suspected, fifteen minutes later Cam spotted Honey making her way over in his direction.

"So you come up in my party and you can't even speak?" Honey asked Cam while looking the two women that accompanied him up and down and instantly she wasn't impressed.

"Oh we speaking now?" Cam said sarcastically. "Cause we been going for days not speaking. That's what we do now, right?" he asked placing his hand on the ass of one of the chicks he came with, just to piss Honey off even further.

Honey's eyes went from Cam's face down to his hand and then back up to his face. "You got three seconds to take your hand off of this raggedy bitch ass!" she said through clenched teeth. Out of nowhere one of Honey's home girls, a ratchet chick named Candy popped up with a stank look on her face.

"You good over here?" Candy asked looking the chicks that came with Cam up and down. "Cause I ain't had a good fight in a minute," she said kicking off her heels. She had no clue what was going on, but none of that even mattered to Candy. She had a few drinks in her and she was ready to hold her girl Honey down.

"Nah it's quiet," Honey smirked. "These bitches know wassup."

"Who the fuck you calling a bitch!" the brown skin chick who's ass Cam had grabbed snapped. "You must got me fuck up! I don't give a fuck who you are! We can get it popping up in here!"

Without warning Honey drew her hand back and slapped the brown skin chick so hard that one of her earrings went flying across the room. Cam quickly jumped in the middle of the two chicks and held Honey back, keeping her up off of the dark skin chicks ass.

By the time security made it over, Candy and the other girl had their hands locked around each other's throats and both of their shirts were ripped. Big titties and weave flew in every direction as a crowd of spectators cheered them on. Minutes later, security roughly man handled Candy and the other two women and escorted them out of the club.

"This just why you don't need to be drinking," Cam yelled in Honey's face once they were over to the side. "Every time you drink, you start acting like a fucking fool!"

"You just can't do right, can you?" Honey asked giving Cam a sad look.

"You drunk right now and you bugging," Cam said trying to take away from the fact that he had just showed up to the club with two women.

"How you show up to my birthday party with two bitches? I mean really Cam? Is it that serious?" Honey asked doing her best not to cry. "Do you love me for real?"

"Listen," Cam began. "I haven't heard from you in days and you have the nerve to ask me do I love you... You bugged out," he said taking the pressure off of him and placing it back on Honey. "You always talking about me, but what have you been doing for these past few days that you've been M.I.A.?"

"Trying to get my head together so I don't snap and kill you," Honey said in a serious tone. "I swear to God, you be trying my patience sometimes. I think you want me to kill one of these little raggedy bitches that you be running around with."

"Speaking of killing," Cam said with a raised eyebrow. "Yolanda and Peanut got shot down the other night. You wouldn't know nothing about that would you?"

"Are you asking me did I shoot Yolanda and Peanut?" Honey asked defensively.

"Yes I am," Cam replied. He didn't believe that Honey would take her hatred for Yolanda that far, but he had to be sure. "She got shot after she left our house."

"No I didn't shoot your little girlfriend," Honey told him. "I wish I did though," she mumbled.

"When you coming back home? I miss you." Cam placed a hand on Honey's thigh and she quickly slapped his hand away.

"I have to drop by the house to grab a few of my things, but after that I'm out," Honey said with an attitude.

"You still mad at me?" Cam asked trying to plant a kiss on Honey's neck, but she moved away before his lips got a chance to connect.

"Am I still mad at you?" Honey echoed. "You running around getting other bitches pregnant and you expect me to be happy!?"

She looked him up and down. "Then on top of that, you got the nerve to come to my birthday party with two ratchet looking hoes on your arm!"

"Nah they wasn't ratchet," Cam said quickly defending the two joints he showed up with.

All Honey could do was shake her head with a disappointed look on her face. As bad as she wanted Cam to do right, she was starting to realize that he just didn't want to do right. A commotion at the front entrance grabbed both Honey and Cam's attention. Bright flashes of light danced throughout the dark club, while several women shrieked. The crowd slowly began to part and snake a path towards the VIP area.

Snow walked in the club draped in black leather and heavy jewels. He was flanked by several hard faced men wearing murderous scowls. From the bulge in Snow's waistband, one could tell that he was definitely strapped.

As Snow was being escorted to the VIP section, he spotted Honey from behind his dark shades. Alongside her sat her clown of a manager, Cam. Snow still felt some type of way about the attempted robbery that took place at the studio, but he had been advised by his lawyer to stay off the radar and avoid unnecessary lawsuits, but Snow didn't know how to stay off the radar. So instead of heading to his VIP section, he made a detour and headed straight for Honey's section instead.

"Listen tonight ain't the night," Truck said blocking Snow and his entourage's path. "You come up in here starting some shit and you gonna get carried up out of here," he warned.

A smirk danced on Snow's lips. "Check this out tough guy; I just came to have a word with Honey. I come in peace or either you can leave in pieces, it's up to you."

That last slick comment had Truck ready to put his hands on the fake tough guy that stood before him, but luckily for Snow, Cam stepped in right on time before things went way left.

"What's good? Something I can help you with?" Cam asked.

"Yeah, I came to see if I could have a word with you and Honey," Snow said with a crooked smile on his face.

"I don't see no harm in that." Cam escorted Snow and a few members from his crew over to the sofa where Honey sat with a drink in her hand.

"Nice to see you again," Snow said leaning in to kiss Honey on the cheek. While leaning in he made sure he rubbed his hands discreetly across Honey's thick thighs. "You missed me?" Snow asked as if Cam wasn't sitting right there.

"What do you want?" Honey asked with a slight attitude. It was her birthday, but yet Cam had figured out a way to piss her off as usual.

"I heard somebody blew your man Peanut's head off," Snow said with smile. "Now since he's out of the picture, I was wondering if we could maybe move forward and get some bread together?"

"What did you have in mind?" Cam asked.

Snow helped himself to a drink and then turned and faced Honey. "Honestly I was really interested in working with Honey and Honey only."

"But you know Cam is my manager," Honey pointed out.

"Fuck that bozo," Snow said as if Cam wasn't sitting right there. "You don't need this clown and you know it. Fuck with a real nigga and I'll show you heights you never would have imagined."

"I thought you said that you wanted to talk business?" Cam cut in with much attitude. He wasn't just going to sit back and let Snow continue to disrespect him.

"I am talking business," Snow said slowly sipping from his drink. He turned his gaze back on Honey. "This the era of the power couples. Me and you together, it won't be no stopping us." Just as the words left Snow's mouth, his new single blared through the speakers and turned the club into a frenzy.

Cam hated to admit it, but even he was feeling the song and had no other choice than to bob his head when the beat dropped.

As Snow spoke to Honey, his entourage had to fight to keep drunk women from hopping over the rail trying to get a hug from the rap star.

"I can take your career to the next level; you dig? Leave these clowns alone and come cross over to the winning team." Snow grabbed Honey's hand and caressed it gently.

Honey quickly snatched her hand out of Snow's grip. "I fucks with Cam and that's that!"

Snow shook his head and gave Honey a sad look. "Whenever you change your mind, you know where to find me." He got up and went to lean in to kiss Honey on the cheek, but she jerked her head back before his lips could make contact with her face.

Snow and his entourage looked Cam up and down daring him to make a move before they finally exited the VIP area.

"Yo I'm out," Cam said as he faked like he was about to leave. Honey quickly hopped up and grabbed his arm stopping him from leaving.

"Why you leaving?" Honey asked. "I know you not mad about that clown Snow."

"So this what you been doing while you been missing for a week?" Cam asked trying to reverse the situation and make Honey feel bad. "Now out the blue niggaz is trying to wife you up?"

"Listen Cam it's my birthday and I really don't feel like fighting with you tonight." Honey downed the rest of her drink in one gulp and then quickly refilled her flute. "You treat me like a fucking prostitute and then you wanna get mad when somebody else offers to treat me right."

"How do I treat you like a prostitute?"

"You constantly with the next chick and then when you get caught you wanna turn around and buy me a gift with my *own* money," Honey said giving Cam a sad look. "Then you go out and trick on these bitches with *my* money."

"That's not *your* money! That's *our* money!" Cam corrected her. "I get paid for managing you," he reminded her.

"I'm the one on stage every motherfucking night singing and dancing, not you!"

"Bitch you wouldn't even be where you are today if it wasn't for me!" Cam snapped. "You let these clown ass niggaz gas your head up if you want to."

As the two went back and forth, across from them in the other VIP area they watched as Snow and his crew stood on couches making it rain and enjoying themselves.

"Cam I just want to be happy," Honey said as her eyes began to water.

"Yeah me too," Cam said as he spun off leaving Honey standing there looking stupid and feeling like shit on her birthday.

Honey watched as Cam exited the VIP section. Before he exited the club, Cam went out of his way to get the attention of some big breasted white girl. All Honey could do was shake her head as she watch Cam and the big breasted white girl exit the club together.

The site of Cam leaving the club with another woman caused Honey to see red and murderous thoughts immediately filled her head. Just the thought of Cam fooling around with another woman had her ready to kill. Without thinking twice, Honey shot to her feet and made a beeline straight for the exit with Truck in tow.

Outside in the parking lot Cam sat behind the wheel of his Benz with his hands up the white girl's dress. The louder the white girl moaned, the faster Cam worked his fingers on her love button. "You nasty ass bitch," he growled in the white girl's ear. "After you cum on my fingers I'm going to fuck the shit out of your mouth and you gonna be a good girl and suck the shit outta this big dick right?"

"Yes," the white girl moaned as her body began to shake uncontrollably. Just as the white girl started to cum, the passenger door swung open and Honey violently snatched her out of the passenger's seat by her hair.

"Bitch!" Honey barked as she went to punch the white girl in her face, but luckily for the white girl, Truck stepped in between the two right on time.

"It's not worth it," Truck warned as he pushed Honey to a comfortable distance. Immediately the white girl took off running through the parking lot not wanting to get caught up in a violent altercation.

"On my birthday!" Honey screamed as she swung on Cam. "You do this to me on my fucking birthday!" She cried as she went to scratch Cam's eyes out, but he quickly grabbed a hold of both of Honey's wrist and restrained her.

"Chill the fuck out!" Cam yelled. "I only did that to make you mad. I knew you were going to come out here and I just wanted some attention from you," he claimed as his hands dropped down to Honey's plump ass.

"You're a fucking liar!" Honey growled. "If I didn't come out here when I did, you'd probably be long stroking that white girl right now!"

"I wanna long stroke you right now," Cam said trying to sneak a kiss, but Honey quickly jerked her head back.

"Nigga please! You ain't long stroking shit over here," Honey said trying to stay strong. The reality of the matter was that she missed Cam like crazy and hadn't had sex since leaving the house and even though Cam was a world class creep, he was a master when it came to pleasing a woman's pussy.

"Come on let's get in the car and go home before it starts raining," Cam said leading Honey around to the passenger door of the Benz. Like the perfect gentleman he opened the door for Honey and helped her inside. He then turned to Truck. "Yo grab her car and meet us at the house," he said as he hopped in the Benz and pulled off.

***

Honey walked through the front door, kicked her heels off, reached up under her shirt from behind and removed her bra, then headed straight for the kitchen where she helped herself to a strong drink. Normally Cam would have said something about her drinking, but tonight since he was already in enough trouble he decided to give Honey a pass.

"You are so sexy when you're mad," Cam said as he rubbed Honey's cheek.

"Fuck you Cam," Honey said downing the liquid fire in one gulp. "I just came here to grab a few of my things and then I'm out."

"What are you so angry for?"

"I'm angry because you make me this way. Oh and don't think for a second that I forgot about you and that blonde hair bitch either!"

"What blonde hair bitch?" Cam asked faking ignorance.

"When I kill the bitch, then you'll know which one I'm talking about!" Honey barked.

Cam crept up on Honey from behind and began to plant soft kisses on the back of her neck. "You don't love me no more?" he asked in a strong whisper as his hands found his way down to Honey's huge ass.

"I hate you Cam," Honey said as her breathing became a little choppy. No matter how mad she was with Cam for some reason she just couldn't seem to resist him.

Cam hiked up Honey's spandex skirt from behind and smiled when he saw that she wasn't wearing any panties. "You still mad at me?" Cam asked as he forced Honey's legs apart and spread both her ass cheeks apart, got down on his knees, dipped his head down and began to slowly lick Honey's clit in a circular motion. Cam heard her breathing change from smooth to desperate and choppy. The sound of Cam's mouth was wet and his determination was loud.

"Oh shit!" Honey moaned. She moaned deep and her body started to shake. She reached her hands back, grabbing a hold of Cam's face steady pulling him deeper into her vagina. She was getting turned on by the slurping that came from between her legs. While Cam worked his tongue, he also slipped two fingers in and out of Honey slowly, only turning her on even more.

"You want me to stop?" Cam teased.

"Fuck me Cam!" Honey begged. "Fuck me!"

"You gonna be a good girl?" Cam asked as his fingers continued to work in and out of Honey.

"Yes daddy I promise I'mma be good… Please fuck me," Honey begged.

Cam spun Honey around, scooped her up in the air, and immediately Honey's thick thighs wrapped around his waist like a pair of pliers. The two kissed passionately as Cam slipped himself inside of Honey's warmth.

"Arrrgh," Honey moaned as Cam split her open entering her walls. She took his heat and he handled her heat in return.

Cam held Honey up with his hands underneath her butt and her legs wrapped around his body. She strained and bounced up and down hard and fast with one arm around Cam's neck and her other palm extended, holding on to the top of the refrigerator to help keep her balance. Cam stroked her hard and fast until she came and when she came, Cam still didn't stop. He kept going until Honey tried to push him away because she couldn't take anymore, but Cam wasn't going anywhere and he wasn't going to be pushed away. He held

Honey in the air and continued to slide in and out of her, held her tight, made her his prisoner. Cam slipped out and Honey moaned and quickly rushed him back inside of her. She grabbed Cam's ass forcing him deeper and deeper inside of her. Her breathing was as thick as the heat between her legs. Her fingernails dug into Cam's skin marking him.

Cam carried Honey over to the leather sofa and sat down. Honey pushed Cam and made him sit back resting on his elbows while she hurried and bounced on top of him with force moving in her own urgent and labored rhythm. She moved like she was no longer in charge of her body. Honey wrapped her arms around Cam's neck and announced her orgasm. He jerked and groaned, fought fire with fire, a battle that he was losing one pant at a time. Cam pounded her, pounded her and stared into her eyes until finally he blew his load.

"Arrrggh!" Cam groaned as his body jerked and then went limp. "Damn!"

Honey quickly hopped up off of Cam with a serious look on her face. "I know you didn't just cum inside of me."

"Sorry baby I just couldn't help myself," Cam said with a devilish grin on his face.

"You know I stopped taking birth control," she said as she rushed towards the bathroom. Minutes later Honey returned from the bathroom with a frown on her face.

"What I do now?" Cam asked with an exhausted look on his face.

"I'm still mad with you," Honey admitted. She loved Cam with all she had, but she couldn't understand why he made her an option when she made him a priority.

"I love you."

"Do you really love me Cam?" Honey asked. "And I mean really, really love me?"

Cam sat silent for a second and then he finally replied. "I do."

"Damn it took you that long to answer if you love me or not?" Honey asked with an attitude.

"Stop acting like that. You know I love you. Now go in the kitchen and make a nigga something to eat," Cam said as he slapped Honey on the ass.

With that being said, Honey headed in the kitchen and began preparing Cam a meal.

"NO WHERE TO RUN"

B londie laid across her bed butt naked staring up at the ceiling listening to Drake's latest CD. Her head was all over the place. She hadn't seen or heard from Cam since his last visit when he put his hands on her. Blondie had reached out several times trying to get in contact with Cam, but to no avail. She was beginning to wonder if Cam even cared about her the way he claimed he did. Every time her phone rang she would break her neck trying to get to it in hopes that it was Cam.

"Fuck this," Blondie said. She was sick and tired of sitting around waiting and hoping that Cam called. She grabbed her iPhone and dialed Cam's number. It rung twice and then the voicemail picked up. Blondie was getting ready to leave Cam a nasty message letting him know how she really felt when she heard what sounded like shattering glass coming from downstairs. Immediately she sat up and turned off the music so she could hear better.

Blondie stood completely still for ten seconds listening for noises. Just as she got ready to breathe a sigh of relief she heard what sounded like a boot stepping on crunched glass. She quickly hopped out of her bed and eased her way over towards the doorway and then inched out into the hallway. As Blondie reached the hallway she heard more and more movement coming from downstairs. "Whoever is down there better leave now!" she yelled. "I have a gun and I'm not afraid to use it!" she lied hoping that her bluff would scare off whoever had broken into her home.

Blondie stood at the top of the stairs when she spotted two mask men charging full speed up the stairs. She couldn't quite make out what they held in their hands, but whatever it was, it was shiny.

Blondie quickly took off in a full sprint back to her bedroom where she slammed and locked the door behind her. Then she ran over to her dresser and struggled as she used all of her might to push it in front of the bedroom door. Seconds later, the sound of someone trying to kick the door open could be heard.

BOOM!

BOOM!

BOOM!

Blondie scrambled over to the bed where her iPhone lay. Her nerves were so bad that it took her two tries before she finally dialed the correct numbers to 911.

"911 how can I help you?" the operator asked.

"Someone's broke into my house and trying to kill me!" Blondie said with her voice full of panic.

"Calm down ma'am. Are you in the house alone?"

BOOM!

BOOM!

With each second that passed the kicks to the door were getting louder and louder.

"Yes! Please send somebody over here now, please!" Blondie begged.

"Help is on the way. Just remain calm and find some place to hide until help arrives," the operator said in a calm tone.

Blondie looked around her room and the only place for her to hide was in the closet. Without thinking twice she ran and hid in the closet and began to pray. Praying wasn't something that Blondie usually did, but right now prayer was all she had. A loud boom startled Blondie as she heard footsteps moving around inside her bedroom. Silent tears slid down her cheeks as the small light under the closet door suddenly became dark.

The closet door was snatched open and on the other side stood two mask men.

"Please don't hurt me," Blondie begged.

Without warning the taller gunman snatched Blondie to her feet by her hair while the shorter gunman shoved a sharp knife in her gut and then twisted the handle back and forth for good measures. The shorter gunman stabbed Blondie repeatedly even after he was sure that she was dead.

***

Detective Washington exited the liquor store and slid back inside his unmarked car. After a long day, he badly needed a drink. Detective Washington was one of the best detective's in the city. He was a detective that took his job serious and he always had a no nonsense attitude when it came to people breaking the law.

Detective Washington cracked open his bottle of Vodka and took a deep swig. Then he heard the dispatcher on his radio announce a home invasion not too far from his location. He took another swig from the bottle as he thought about ignoring the call and heading home, but the cop in him wouldn't allow him to go home.

"10-4, I'm not too far away from that location. I'll go check it out," Detective Washington said into his walkie-talkie as he headed towards the address.

When Detective Washington arrived at the location the bottle of Vodka he'd been drinking was almost half empty. He looked at the town house and nothing looked out of the ordinary. "Fuck," he cursed as he slid out of the driver door and headed towards the front door of the house.

Detective Washington stopped short when he saw the front door ajar and broken glass near the entrance. "Detective Washington requesting back up," he whispered into his walkie-talkie as he whipped his 9mm out of the holster with a snap. Detective Washington held his 9mm with a strong two handed grip as he eased his way towards the front door. The smart thing to do would have been to wait for his back up, but that's not how Detective Washington operated. If someone inside the house was really in danger, they would more than likely be dead before back up arrived and that was a risk that he wasn't willing to take.

Detective Washington took his right hand and eased the front door open, when two bullets exploded through the door blowing thick chunks of wood inches away from his face.

"Shit!" Detective Washington cursed as he entered the house on the silent count of three. When he entered the house he spotted a man in all black flee out the back door before he got a chance to get a shot off. He immediately took off behind the gunman. When Detective Washington made it out the back door he spotted two men running in opposite directions. Having to make a split decision, Detective Washington decided to go after the taller of the two gunmen.

The tall gunman hopped a nearby fence and dashed out into the woods.

Detective Washington hopped the fence and went after the gunman. His motto was to shoot and ask questions later especially since the gunmen were armed and dangerous. As he ran through the woods, he heard the sound of several different guns being blasted coming from the direction that the other gunman had headed, indicating that his backup had arrived.

Detective Washington sprinted blindly through the woods. He had no idea where he was headed, but what he did know was that there was no way that he was letting the gunman get away.

The gunman zipped through the woods like an expert. He had no clue where the path in the woods would lead him. His main concern was not getting caught. As he ran, he threw his arm over his shoulder and fired off five reckless shots in the direction of the detective in an attempt to slow him down. Up ahead the gunman spotted an abandoned looking house. With him running out of breath, he had no choice but to enter the abandoned house.

Detective Washington took cover behind a tree, trying to avoid the bullets that he heard zipping through the leaves on the trees. Whoever these gunmen were, it was obvious that jail wasn't an option. If they were caught, they planned on holding court in the street.

Detective Washington inched his way towards the front door of the abandoned house. He took a deep breath then came forward and kicked the front door open. He quickly removed his flashlight and slowly entered the house. With one hand Detective Washington held a firm grip on his gun and with his other hand; he held a tight grip on the flashlight. Movement coming from upstairs grabbed Detective Washington's attention. Without thinking twice he headed upstairs in the direction of the noise. Detective Washington's eyes were having a hard time adjusting to the dark, not to mention he had no clue what was lying around the next corner. He eased through the abandoned house with the business end of his gun leading the way. The wood floor squeaking caused Detective Washington to spin around and when he looked up, he saw the tall gunman swing a two by four at his face and then suddenly everything went black.

"WHERE AM I"

D etective Washington woke up surrounded by paramedics and police officers. He was quickly helped up to his feet by a uniformed officer that he'd seen around a few times. "Did ya'll catch the gunman?" was the first thing Detective Washington asked.

"No sorry he got away," the officer replied.

"What about the second gunman?"

"They both got away."

"Any clues?" Detective Washington asked as he exited the abandoned house and headed back towards the victims townhouse. He was pissed off that he had let the gunman get away.

"No clues," the officer said. "But we did check the victims phone records and the last call she made was to a Mr. Cameron Johnson."

"Really?" Detective Washington said as his eyes lit up.

"Yes, the one that manages that chick with the huge ass. I think her name is Honey," the officer said.

"I know exactly who he is," Detective Washington said as he quickly hopped in his car and peeled off.

***

The tall gunman reached the safe house and was glad to see his partner sitting down on the couch enjoying a glass of wine. The two smiled and hugged one another.

"Glad you made it back in one piece. Were you followed?" the shorter gunman asked.

"Nah I'm good," the tall man replied.

"Alright. Change your clothes and get cleaned up so we can get out of here. We got a lot of more work to put in," the short gunman said with a smile. The gunman never knew how much fun it would be to take a person's life until he actually did it. After the first kill, it was hard to turn off the adrenaline rush. Killing was now becoming a sport or some sort of challenge that just had to be fulfilled.

"JEALOUSY"

A fter everything that had went down the night of Honey's birthday, Cam had been trying to do better, but being good was beginning to be too much work. He called himself doing the right thing so he could get out of the dog house. Cam sat on the couch with his feet kicked up watching ESPN, but his mind was elsewhere. Cam's mind was stuck on Yolanda's new friend that he ran into at the hospital. He couldn't believe that Yolanda would violate by having another man in her hospital room instead of him. It bothered him even more that the diesel dude really seemed to care for Yolanda's wellbeing. Immediately Cam's mind began to think that Yolanda probably had been messing around with diesel nigga the whole time. What really pissed Cam off was the fact that Yolanda had moved on and that she may even be falling in love with this new man. The falling in love part pissed him off even further. The sound of Honey's heels stabbing the hard wood floor snapped Cam out of his thoughts.

"Hey what are you over here thinking about?" Honey asked standing in front of Cam wearing nothing but a pair of expensive heels that she couldn't even pronounce the name of. Right above her pussy lips was a fresh tattoo that read "CAM".

"What's that?" Cam asked.

"What does it look like?" Honey countered looking at Cam like he was crazy. "It's your name!"

Cam placed a fake smile on his face. He planned on breaking away from Honey as soon as he found the next superstar in the making so her tattoo really meant nothing to him, but he decided to play along. "I love it! Thanks baby," he said as he stood up and kissed her on the lips and palmed her ass.

"I love you to death! You know that right?" Honey asked looking Cam in his eyes. "You know that I would kill you before I let you leave me right?"

"Here you go with that crazy shit again," Cam huffed as he tried to push away from Honey, but she held him tight.

"I'm serious Cam. You are stuck with me forever!" Honey smiled to hide the fact that she was extremely serious and meant every word that she said. "I'll never let you be happy with the next woman... Never!" she said as she reached down and grabbed Cam's dick. "This is all my dick!"

Not in the mood to argue, Cam just agreed with whatever Honey was rambling about. The only thing that was on his mind at the moment was Yolanda and her new diesel boyfriend.

"I know just what you need," Honey said clearing off the coffee table with a swipe of her hand. She laid Cam down on the coffee table as she quickly removed his sweatpants and stared at his dick that stood at attention. Honey sexily walked around towards the other end of the coffee table where Cam's head resided. "I got something for you," she purred as she straddled his face backwards. Cam quickly craned his neck up and began to slowly and expertly lick and slurp on Honey's sweet pussy.

"Ahhh," Honey moaned as she gyrated her hips and gave Cam's face a nice slow ride. Nothing turned Cam on more than making a woman have an orgasm. His slurping became even more intense when he felt Honey's lips wrap around his dick. Right there on the coffee table the two pleased each other orally in the perfect 69 position. The faster Cam slurped, the more Honey sucked. Honey gripped Cam's dick with two hands and began jerking, twisting her hands, and sucking all in one motion as she grinding her hips even further into Cam's face. She loved how he licked her pussy, loved how he took his time to satisfy and please her, and loved how he made it his business to make sure her orgasm was explosive, and most importantly she loved how he sucked on her pussy like his life depended on it. "OH MY FUCKING GOD!!!!" Honey screamed as her orgasm took over and flooded Cam's mouth and nose. A loud knock at the door startled the couple and interrupted their sex session.

Cam sat up, wiped off his mouth, put his sweatpants back on, and then headed over towards the door. Whoever was knocking at the door was acting as if it was an emergency of some sort. Cam looked through the peephole and sucked his teeth. He opened the door and on the other side stood Detective Washington along with several other officers. "Fuck you want?" Cam asked as if the detective's presence was an annoyance.

"You're under arrest for the murder of Nancy O'neil," Detective Washington said as he slapped the cuffs on Cam's wrist. He didn't have any evidence, but he needed to get Cam downtown in order to question him.

"Yo, get my lawyer on the phone!" Cam yelled to Honey as Detective Washington shoved him in the backseat of the squad car. Just as they were about to pull off, the media pulled up and began to surround the property trying to be first to break the story.

Honey quickly ran inside the house and called Cam's lawyer. She didn't have a clue what was going on, all she heard the detective say was murder. Honey felt as if her heart was about to stop. Just the thought of Cam having to do life in prison caused her to go into panic mode.

"Truck!" Honey called out.

Like magic Truck seemed to appear out of nowhere.

"I need you to drive me to the precinct," Honey said in a fast tone. The only thing that covered her body was a towel that she had quickly grabbed from one of the guest bathrooms when she first heard the loud knock at the door. She quickly ran upstairs, threw on a long sun dress, some sandals, threw her hair in a loose ponytail, and then ran back down stairs.

Truck pushed his way pass all the media and news reporters until he reached the all black Escalade. He helped Honey in the back seat, hopped behind the wheel, and headed straight for the precinct.

"INTERROGATION"

C am sat in an empty room with nothing but a table and chair. He'd been in the custody of the police for over four hours now and he still hadn't seen anyone. Just as Cam got ready to rest his head on the table and take a cat nap, he heard the door open and in stepped Detective Washington.

"What the fuck am I doing here?" Cam asked with an attitude. He had bette r things to be doing with his time than to be sitting around playing games with the dumb ass police.

"Can you explain your relations with Nancy O'neil?" Detective Washington asked helping himself to a seat across from Cam.

"She's a chick who I smashed from time to time. Is it a crime to smash chicks nowadays?"

"Not at all, but it is a crime if after you smash them, you kill them," Detective Washington said with a raised brow. "It seems like every female connected to you ends up getting killed or seriously wounded," he pointed out. "You wouldn't know why that is, now would you?"

Cam shook his head. "Nope."

"Sure you don't," Detective Washington smiled. He knew Cam was full of shit and he couldn't wait until he had a reason to arrest him.

"Now if you're done wasting my time, can I get going?"

"We're done when I say we're done motherfucker!" Detective Washington growled. "First Yolanda and now Nancy A.K.A. Blondie. Who's next Cam? How long are you going to allow innocent people to keep getting hurt?"

"What the fuck you want me to do? You acting like I'm the one out here killing these woman!" Cam spat.

"Are you?" Detective Washington asked with a raised brow. "Are you the one out here killing these women?"

"No!"

"Well if it's not you, then you must know who's responsible for these heinous acts," Detective Washington huffed. "And I'm going to need your help tracking them down."

"Why did you say murders, when it's only been one murder?" Cam shook his head. "You want me to help you do your job," he laughed. "Fuck you!"

"Well whoever is out here trying to kill these woman, it's only going to be a matter of time before they come after you, but then it'll be too late," Detective Washington said smiling.

Cam faked a yawn. "Am I free to go?"

"Yes you are," Detective Washington said standing to his feet. "See you around."

"Fuck you," Cam said as he spun past the detective. Several hours of his life had just been wasted for nothing. He felt bad that Blondie had been murdered, but what could he do about it? It wasn't like he knew who was responsible for taking her life. What really pissed Cam off was that he had missed a meeting with this new R&B chick who was on the come up named Bambi. Bambi was the next superstar in the making and she badly wanted to work with Cam, but now because of this foolishness he had missed his meeting with the new talent.

When Cam stepped out of the precinct, he was happy to see Honey leaning up against her Escalade with a smile on her face. At times Cam may have disliked Honey, but one thing that was for sure was this chick was a rider. She proved to him time and time again that she had his back to the fullest under any circumstances and for that reason alone, Cam not only loved Honey, but he respected her.

"Hey daddy," Honey sang as she ran and jumped in Cam's arms. "Why the fuck was those crackers harassing my man?"

Cam sucked his teeth. "Talking some silly murder shit," he said as him and Honey slid in the back seat of the Escalade.

"Who got murdered?" Honey asked.

"Some chick that I knew," Cam said brushing it off.

"Why would they think that you murdered her?"

"I have no idea," Cam lied. It was no way that he was going to tell Honey that the woman that had been murdered was the same woman that she had been complaining about and the reason he was being questioned was because he was the last person that she had tried to call before she was murdered. "I missed my meeting I had with that new singer chick."

"Who Bambi?" Honey spat, her voice full of jealousy.

"Yeah, I seen a few of her videos on YouTube. I think with my help she can go to the top," Cam said.

"Mmmm...Hmmm...," Honey hummed. "Cam I swear you and her better do straight business and no funny shit cause just like any other bitch, I'll whip her ass too."

"Here we go," Cam huffed. "Why can't you just sit down and chill? Why you always have to be threatening someone?"

* * *

"The same reason every time I turn around you smiling all up in a bitch face!" Honey spat. She was tired of playing games with Cam and she wanted it to be known that she had no problem acting a fool if she had to. "Keep these little microwaveable bitches in they place and we won't have no problems. See how easy that was."

Instead of going back and forth with Honey about nothing, Cam decided to just agree with whatever she said as he helped himself to a drink. He drank straight out of the bottle like a savage. Cam pulled out his phone and sent Bambi an email apologizing for missing their meeting and he asked if they could meet one day later in the week. Almost instantly he got a response back from Bambi saying that she would love to meet another day. Cam slid his phone back down in his pocket and sat back and enjoyed a nice drink while Honey slipped her hand down his sweatpants and played with his dick for the rest of their ride home. When Cam felt his dick about to explode, he leaned forward and told Truck to keep his eyes on the road and out of the rearview mirror as he grabbed the back of Honey's head and shoved her face down in his lap.

"I DON'T LIKE YOU"

C am sat on the couch having a drink while Honey danced around the living room singing "Drunk In Love," by Beyonce. Cam had just finished giving Honey the fucking of a lifetime so needless to say, she was feeling good and in a good mood.

"We be all night!" Honey sang along with Beyonce as she began mimicking the same dance moves that Beyonce had performed in the video. Cam did his best to pay Honey no mind. At the moment he had bigger and better things on his mind like Yolanda. What was she doing and who was she doing it with? Ever since the hospital incident Cam hadn't heard one word from Yolanda and just the thought of her being happy with someone else pissed him off. In his mind he thought that Yolanda would wait around forever for him, but now that she was gone and had really moved on, it bothered him.

"Come sing and dance with me baby," Honey said trying to pull Cam up off the couch.

"Nah I'm good," Cam quickly declined as he stood to his feet. "I'll be back in a second," he said and then headed to the door.

"Where you going?" Honey asked nosily.

"To the store," Cam lied. "I'll be right back."

"Don't forget I got a walked through at that club in three hours," Honey reminded him.

"I'll be back way before then," Can said and then was out the door. Cam slid behind the wheel of his B.M.W. and headed straight for Yolanda's house. He had some questions that needed to be answered. He needed to know what was really going on. Millions of different scenarios played out in his mind while he drove. Deep down inside Cam still loved Yolanda and he would rather die before seeing her with another man.

Cam pulled up to the house and immediately became angry when he saw two cars parked in the driveway. *"This bitch must have lost her mind,"* he said to himself as he slid out the Beemer and headed towards the front door. Cam pulled out his key, opened the front door, and walked straight inside the house.

Cam walked through the house until he spotted Yolanda's new boyfriend Richard sitting at the table romantically feeding Yolanda pasta with a fork as if she was a baby. By the delicate and loving manner that he was feeding Yolanda Cam could tell that the two were more than just *"friends"*.

Cam cleared his throat loudly grabbing Yolanda and Richard's attention. "Hope I'm not interrupting anything," he said with his voice full of jealously.

"Cam!" Yolanda yelled jumping up with a startled and embarrassed look on her face. "What are you doing here?"

"This is my house. What do you mean what am I doing here?" Cam replied. "The question is what is *he* doing here?"

"We were just having dinner, and..."

"Baby you ain't gotta explain shit to him!" Richard said jumping in the conversation cutting Yolanda off. He quickly positioned Yolanda behind him as if he was protecting her. "Listen you clown!" Richard barked. "I'm sick and tired of you coming around trying to ruin me and Yolanda's relationship. She's moved on and you need to respect that!"

Cam looked at Yolanda's diesel new boy toy like he had lost his mind. "Check this out my man," Cam said in a calm tone. "I wasn't even talking to you and I'd appreciate it if you'd shut the fuck up and mind your business before you get hurt," he said and then turned his attention to Yolanda who stood behind Richard with a scared look on her face. Yolanda could tell that Cam was drunk. She prayed that he would just leave before somebody got hurt.

"How you gonna have another man in the house that I paid for?" Cam asked looking Yolanda up and down with a disgusted look on his face.

"Cam I've given you seven years of my life and all you've done was take advantage of me and take my kindness for..."

"Bitch get your shit and get the fuck out!" Cam snapped cutting Yolanda off. He wasn't pissed that Yolanda had another man, what he was really pissed about was the fact that Yolanda was officially over him and she had officially broken away from him. "I should of known you was a hoe," Cam said shaking his head.

"You can't stand to see me happy can you?" Yolanda said.

Cam looked Yolanda up and down. "You disgust me," he said with passion.

Yolanda's eyes began to water. The way Cam was talking to her made her feel real small. "Fine! I'm getting my things and I'm leaving!" she yelled.

"And hurry up! It smells like a hoe house up in here," Cam said with a smirk on his face.

"Watch how you talk to my lady and I ain't gonna tell you again!" Richard said with his voice full of rage. He told himself that he was going to stay out of this mess, but Cam was taking the name calling and insults a little too far. It had gotten to the point where he had to step in.

"And what the fuck you going to do if I don't?" Cam asked taking a threatening step forward. His jealously had officially gotten the best of him and it was too high to be turned off now.

Richard laughed as he removed his shirt revealing his muscular frame. His body looked like Hulk Hogan's in his prime. "I'm from the old school and I ain't never been the type to walk away from a good fight."

Yolanda thought about stepping in before things went too far, but then she said fuck it. She was tired of Cam always trying to steal her joy and she badly wanted to see him get his ass whipped. "Take him outside and knock his stupid ass out!" Yolanda cheered from the sideline as she watched the two men head outside to the front lawn.

Cam stood outside waiting for the muscle man to come out. Even though he was a little tipsy he still wasn't worried about the muscular man. From his experiences when he used to get into street fights, Cam found out that most guys with big muscles couldn't fight worth a damn. All they were good at was grabbing and wrestling. As Cam stood there waiting, Richard came storming out of the house running full speed trying to catch Cam off guard. Cam quickly fired off two punches that landed on the top of Richard's head as he tackled Cam like a linebacker lifting him up off his feet and then driving him down hard onto the ground. Richard landed on top of Cam and quickly positioned himself in between Cam's legs UFC style and began to pound away at Cam's face. Cam did his best to fight the big man off, but the weight difference was turning into a bigger problem than he expected.

***

Detective Washington sat staked out across the street from Yolanda's house because it seemed like everyone who came close to Cam ended up dying. Detective Washington planned on getting to the bottom of the murders and discovering who was behind all the cruel and gruesome attacks. The next closest person to Cam was Yolanda so Detective Washington decided to stakeout her house in hopes that the killer showed up there next and if they did, he would have something waiting for them. As Detective Washington sat in his car sipping from a bottle of Vodka, he noticed a car pull up. At first he thought it was the killer showing up to finish Yolanda off. Detective Washington quickly snatched his gun from his holster and got ready to hop out the car, until he saw Cam hop out the car.

He breathed a sigh of relief and slid his gun back inside his holster and continued to get his sip on. If his hunch was right, then he knew sooner or later the killer would show up to finish the job that they started on Yolanda. Detective Washington went to take another swig from his bottle when he spotted Cam exit the house and seconds later he spotted Yolanda's new boyfriend from the hospital charge out the house and tackle Cam down to the ground. At first Detective Washington was about to jump out his car and break up the fight, but then he decided against it. Cam needed a good ass whipping so why should he stand in the way of that?

Detective Washington got out of his car and leaned up against the hood and enjoyed the show. At first he was laughing until he felt that Cam had, had enough. Detective Washington jogged over towards the front lawn and quickly got Richard up off of Cam. He then escorted Cam over towards his car.

"This shit ain't over motherfucker!" Cam yelled just to save face. The truth was, he wanted no more parts of the brolic man. It had been a long time since he'd taken an ass whipping like that.

"Why are you over here causing trouble?" Detective Washington barked. "You want me to take your ass to jail?"

"Take me to jail for what? This is my house!" Cam snapped. He hated to be petty, but there was no way he was going to allow a man to stay in a house that he had paid for. "What time is it?"

"2:30 a.m.," Detective Washington answered.

"Fuck!" Cam cursed. He was supposed to meet Honey for her walk through at1 a.m. He automatically knew that, that was a fight just waiting to happen when he got home.

"PISSED OFF"

oney sat in the VIP section of the club with a bottle of wine in her hand. She was pissed off to the tenth power that Cam had mysteriously gone missing. The first thing that came to her mind was him and another woman. His track record was so bad that even if he was out doing right, it would always look, feel, and seem like he was out doing wrong. Immediately Honey's mind went to how she was going to smack the shit out of Cam when she caught up with him. She was sick and tired of Cam playing her for a fool. Truck's strong voice snapped Honey out of her thoughts.

"You know this fool?" Truck asked pointing to a slim framed man who was sporting a pair of nerd glasses.

"Yeah he cool," Honey said. The skinny man in the glasses was Marcus. Marcus was an old friend of hers who used to promote parties. Before she got famous he always got Honey in the club without having to wait in the long ass lines. He was one of the first people to treat Honey like a celebrity before she actually became a celebrity.

"Hey Marcus how have you been?" Honey asked with a smile.

"Much better now that I'm here with you," Marcus capped back as he sat down and helped himself to a drink. He had been madly in love with Honey ever since he had first met the beautiful woman a few years ago.

"What brings you to the club tonight?" Honey asked yelling over the loud bass that bumped from the speakers.

"I heard you were going to be here so I figured why not swing by and say hello," Marcus said with a smile. He slickly let his hand slip down to Honey's voluptuous thigh.

"Awww how sweet," Honey said as she nicely removed his hand from her thigh. Marcus was nowhere near Honey's type, but even if he was, there was no way that she would cheat on Cam. Even though she knew she should have been kicked his cheating ass to the curb.

"When you going to let me take you out?" Marcus asked. "I mean I know I'm not rich or nothing, but I do pretty good for myself," he said as if he was trying to convince himself more than Honey.

"Marcus you know I'm in a relationship," Honey told him. She hoped and prayed that he'd take the hint so she wouldn't have to hurt his feelings and embarrass him.

"You still with that same cat?" Marcus asked with his face crumbled up. "That same cat that had you out fighting in the streets that last time?"

"Yup that's him," Honey said taking a swig from her bottle. She knew Marcus was trying to take a shot at her, but she decided to hold her tongue just this once. She didn't want to hurt Marcus's feelings but if he tried to get slick again, Honey planned on letting him have it.

"You know I've been feeling you for a while. Why don't you let me take you out one time and see what it's like to be treated like a woman for once instead of some hoe," Marcus said and then took a sip from his drink.

He wasn't trying to be disrespectful, but being nice was obviously getting him nowhere.

"Listen Marcus I think you're a nice guy, but you are just not my type," Honey said as nice as possible. "I'm pretty sure you'll find the one for you."

"You bitches are crazy!" Marcus huffed. "A good man come along that's willing to treat you right, but you'd still rather stay with someone that treats you like shit! I just don't get it!"

Honey was trying to be nice, but she just couldn't take it anymore. "Listen I was trying to be nice, but honestly you a clown and quite frankly I don't do clowns!"

"Hmmp," Marcus huffed looking Honey up and down like she was trash. "You bum ass bitches kill me! Niggaz get on T.V. and start acting like they better than niggaz! I remember when you used to beg me to get you in the club and for free might I add, but now that you got a little bit of money, I'm a clown? I guess you don't have any mirrors in your mansion!"

Honey was about to call Truck over so he could slap the taste out of Marcus' mouth, but he must have felt the tension in the air because he quickly got up and walked off mumbling something under his breath. Honey was sick and tired of clowns thinking just because they came from the same place, that they were all equal. Honey's cell phone buzzing stole her attention. She looked down at her phone and saw Cam's name flashing across the screen. Honey sucked her teeth, hit the ignore button, and then tossed her phone down in her purse. At that moment she wasn't in the mood to deal with Cam and his bullshit.

Honey was taking a swig from her bottle of wine when she saw a big man climb over the VIP velvet ropes screaming, "I love you Honey" at the top of his lungs. From the look in the big man's eyes, Honey could tell that he wasn't going to try to hurt her, he had the star struck look of a man who had never seen a celebrity in real life before. The big man stuck his hand out for a hand shake, but before he could fully extend his hand, Truck had already tackled the big man down to the floor.

Over on the other side of the club an altercation broke out and shortly after three shots rang out.

Bang! Bang! Bang!

Immediately the entire club turned into a frenzy as everyone rushed and tried to scramble out of the main exit. At first Honey didn't react to the gunshots, but when she heard more gunshots, she quickly kicked off her heels, grabbed them from off the floor, and ran in a low crouch towards the exit. After pushing and shoving, Honey finally made it out to the parking lot. As she ran through the parking lot, she heard four more shots ring out followed by loud screams.

Bang! Bang! Bang! Bang!

As Honey ran through the parking lot, she heard a set of footsteps coming up on her from behind. She spun around in fear and then breathed a sigh of relief when she saw that it was just Marcus. "Damn Marcus you scared the shit out of me!"

Without warning Marcus turned and slapped Honey down to the ground.

Honey looked from the ground and watched as Marcus removed a gun from his waist and aimed it at her. "Marcus what the fuck are you doing?"

"Who the fuck is the clown now!?" Marcus growled through clenched teeth. He quickly reached down and snatched the chain from around Honey's neck. "Run that bracelet and them ear rings too!"

"You're making a big mistake Marcus. Trust me you don't want to do..." A kick to the ribs interrupted Honey's sentence and silenced her.

"Bitch shut the fuck up!" Marcus barked as he reached down and snatched Honey's purse from off the ground. He looked down at Honey, smiled, and then dramatically cleared his throat and spit right in Honey's face before he took off in a sprint in the opposite direction of the club.

"I swear to God I'm going to kill that motherfucker!" Honey said to herself as she wiped the saliva mixed with phlegm from her face and pulled herself up from off the ground.

"VALENTINES DAY"

C am sat parked in his Benz directly in front of his studio. The reason he sat in the car was because he was supposed to be meeting Bambi at the studio today and at the moment he was on the phone with Honey. He wanted to talk to her before he entered the studio just in case he had to flirt with the beautiful singer in order to get her to sign with his company and he couldn't allow Honey to hear that so he figured why not get her out of the way before he entered the studio.

"Yes baby," Cam said into the phone.

"Yes what?"

"I know it is Valentine's Day and I promise I won't be home late."

"You better get here at a decent time because I want to go out to eat and maybe go and check out that new Kevin Hart movie," Honey said smiling on the other end of the phone. "Oh and I want chocolate, roses, a teddy bear, and all that good shit."

"You got it baby. Now let me get going and handle this business so I can get back at a reasonable time," Cam told her.

"Okay baby go handle your business and you better not be flirting with that Bambi bitch either," Honey spat. "And let that bitch know that she better not try to come at my man sideways because I have no problem mopping the floor with her ass!"

Cam shook his head, hung up his phone, and grabbed his .380 from under the seat before exiting the Benz. After Honey told him what Marcus had done to her the other night, he planned on making an example of him whenever the two crossed paths.

When Cam entered the lobby of his studio, he spotted a beautiful woman dressed in a tight baby blue dress that stopped just above her thighs. Her lips were painted in bright red lipstick.

"Well hello Mr. Cam," Bambi said with a smile as she sized Cam up. Bambi favored the actress LisaRaye McCoy. "For a second I thought that you were going to stand me up."

"Now why would I do something like that?" Cam opened his arms for a hug. When their bodies made contact, Cam inhaled Bambi's sweet scent and immediately he felt his dick jump. Cam quickly released her and they walked over to the elevator. In the elevator, the two checked one another out and openly flirted with the other.

"Imma fuck the shit out that pussy as soon as we get upstairs," Cam said to himself as they exited the elevator.

"It's a pleasure to finally meet you," Bambi said helping herself to a seat on an expensive looking chair. "You look ten times better in person than you do on T.V."

"Is that right?" Cam asked as he pulled out a bottle of Ciroc and poured him and Bambi both a drink.

"So super manager," Bambi said smiling. "Why were you so interested in meeting me?"

"Because I know I can take you all the way to the top just like I did Honey." Cam took a sip from his drink. "You have the looks, the drive, the hustle, and not to mention your voice is amazing."

"So is it true what I been hearing on T.V.?" Bambi asked. She crossed one of her legs on top of the other causing her dress to rise even higher.

"T.V. and social media is the devil," Cam replied as his eyes landed on Bambi's thick thighs. He tried to shake the crazy sexual thoughts from his brain, but the task was more difficult than he expected.

"I'm going to cut straight to the chase are you and Honey an item?" Bambi asked.

Cam thought about lying, but he knew there was no way for him to keep him and Honey's relationship a secret so instead he didn't give Bambi a straight answer. "Something like that."

Bambi smiled and removed her shoes revealing her pretty feet. "Sorry, but these shoes are new and I haven't broken them in yet."

"What about you? Are you in a relationship?" Cam asked.

"Something like that," Bambi said smiling. The sexual tension that was in the air was thick enough to cut with a knife. "Let's talk about this contract. I have a few questions."

"Ask away."

"Benefits?" Bambi smiled. "What type of benefits do I get if I sign this contract?"

Cam quickly read between the lines. He could tell that Bambi was feeling him and wanted him to fuck her brains out, but he played it cool. "Depends on what type of benefits you talking about."

"I'm talking about the same type of benefits that Honey is getting."

"Depends," Cam replied.

"On what?"

"On if you're worth the benefits. Not just anybody that signs with me get those type of benefits," Cam said with a raised brow.

"I see," Bambi said as she uncrossed her legs and spread them apart. "You wanna eat my pussy don't you?"

The question caught Cam off guard, but he had to play it cool. "Excuse me?"

"I said you want to eat my pussy don't you!" Bambi repeated in a strong, sexy, porn star type of voice as she spread her legs open even further.

Cam didn't say a word. He just nodded his head up and down indicating he was saying yes.

"I can't hear you!"

"I said yes."

"Yes what?"

"Yes I want to eat your pussy," Cam said.

Bambi hiked her dress up revealing that she wasn't wearing any panties as she spread her legs and rested them on the arms of the chair. "Get over here!" she said through clenched teeth. She placed both of her hands on the back of Cam's head and gripped it tightly and shoved his face down into her pussy.

Moans that started off slow become desperate. "Oh my God!" Bambi moaned with her head hung back over the chair. Cam expertly licked Bambi's clit like a kitten drinking milk as he slipped two fingers inside her love tunnel. When he reached her g-spot, he made a *come here* gesture with his fingers. He did that repeatedly as his tongue worked fifty miles per hour simultaneously.

"Ooo... Ooo.... Oohhh... Oh Shit! Oh my God!" Bambi screamed as her legs began to shake uncontrollably. She moaned, cursed, and held on to whatever she could hold on to. Her orgasm came hard and fast. It came in a series of waves. "Jesus!" Bambi yelled with her face crumbled up. She noticed that after she had came, Cam was still licking, sucking, and slurping on her swollen clit. "Oh my God! Noooo! I can't take it no more! Please stop!" Bambi jerked, and made sounds that told Cam that she was on fire. Cam quickly stood up, grabbed Bambi's hand and led her over to the piano. Cam sat down on the bench and pulled Bambi down onto his lap backwards and slipped inside of her wet warm slice.

"Sssss..." Bambi moaned as Cam filled her insides with all nine inches of his dick. He slapped Bambi's ass as she bounced up and down. She went up easy and then came down hard with force. Cam watched as Bambi's ass jiggled each time it violently slapped off his torso.

Cam grabbed a hand full of Bambi's hair and roughly jerked her head back so he could suck on her neck.

"Oh my God this dick is so good!" Bambi yelled with her eyes closed tight as she bounced up and down on Cam's dick. Cam reached up and jammed two fingers in Bambi's mouth and began to slide them in and out of her mouth nice and slow. Bambi bounced on Cam's dick like it was a Pogo Stick while sucking the shit out of his fingers all at the same time. She abandoned her lady like ways, her politeness, became sexual and primal, and all without saying a word that Cam could comprehend; she demanded more.

"Cam, Cam, oh shit Cam!" Bambi's legs trembled. Then her entire body did the same as she came all over Cam's dick.

Cam quickly hopped up, sat Bambi down on the bench, and stood in between her legs with his dick standing at attention inches away from Bambi's face. Bambi opened her mouth and leaned in to taste it. Cam quickly took a step back and slapped Bambi across her face with his dick. Then he moved closer and jammed it in her mouth.

"Mmmm..." she moaned as she desperately slurped her juices off of Cam's dick. Then she lifted Cam's dick and gently licked and sucked on his balls the whole time moaning like a phone sex operator.

Bambi removed Cam's dick from her mouth with a loud plop, looked Cam in the eyes and said. "I want you to fuck my mouth!"

A smirk danced on Cam's lips as he gripped Bambi's head with two hands and jammed his dick back in her mouth. He pumped in and out of Bambi's mouth like he was possessed causing Bambi to gag repeatedly. When Cam felt himself getting ready to explode he quickly pulled out and painted Bambi's face with his semen.

Bambi closed her eyes and held her tongue out like a good girl.

"Oooooh shit!" Cam growled as he slipped his dick back in Bambi's mouth. He closed his eyes like he was praying and then grunted. He put his hand down on top of Bambi's head, as he felt her swallowing. She finished and slowed down the passionate sucking and stroking action. A few moments later Bambi raised her head, wiped the sides of her lips, and smiled. "You better not had gotten any in my hair," she said as she scurried off to the bathroom.

Cam sat back with a smile on his face. He could see him and Bambi's relationship lasting for a while as long as Honey didn't destroy it. Just knowing that he was about to make a ton of money off of Bambi was good, but things were even better now that he knew her sex was also the bomb. What Cam saw for his future put a huge smile on his face.

***

In the bathroom Bambi stood staring at her reflection with a frown on her face as she wiped Cam's semen from her face with a warm rag. She hated men like Cam, men who thought that they were God's gift to women, men who felt because they had money that a woman had to put up with all types of bullshit. Little did Cam know, but Bambi had planned on putting an end to all that. It would only be a matter of time before she got pregnant and took Cam for every dime he had. In Bambi's mind that would be payback for all the good women that Cam and men like him had fucked over. Bambi knew men like Cam loved a woman with a nice body and a woman who knew when to shut up. All she had to do was show him a little loyalty and she'd have him eating out of the palm of her hands and before he knew it, she would be pregnant.

Bambi applied a fresh coat of make-up to her face and then joined Cam back out into the studio. "Did you miss me?"

"Maybe," Cam said slyly. In his mind he thought that after fucking Bambi once, she would now be addicted to his dick game and he could now treat her however he wanted.

"You better had missed me," Bambi said sliding down onto Cam's lap. "You left bite marks on my neck, but I covered them up the best I could with my make-up."

"My bad baby. That pussy was so good that I couldn't control myself," Cam admitted.

"My man supposed to be picking me up in about a half," Bambi said.

"Your man?" Cam repeated.

"Yes my man," Bambi said. "I did have a life before I met you."

"Well you going to have to tell your man that you about to be super busy," Cam said with a sinister smile on his face. "And make sure you tell him that me and you going to be spending a lot of time together."

"I don't see no contract," Bambi replied. Then she watched as Cam walked over to a table in the corner of the studio and came back with a thick folder in his hand.

"Here and make sure to let your lawyer look over this," Cam said smiling. "The sooner you sign this the better, cause I have a track already in mind for you," he told her. "We can put your single out and start getting this paper."

"Sounds good to me."

Cam smiled as he pressed a button on the switchboard and then the speakers boomed with a crazy beat. Cam watched as Bambi crumbled up her face and bobbed her head to what she was hearing. Immediately she knew that her voice combined with that beat were sure to make her and Cam a ton of money. "I told you I got you," Cam said palming a hand full of Bambi's ass.

Bambi leaned in and kissed Cam on the lips. "I really appreciate what you doing for me."

"Shit ain't about nothing," Cam said as he heard a loud knock at the door. "Yoooo," he called out. One of his beefy security guards stuck his neck through the door.

"Boss it's some clown ass police out here talking about he's here to pick somebody up. You want me to throw him out?"

Cam was getting ready to say yeah until Bambi quickly hopped up off his lap.

"Yeah let him in. That's my man," Bambi said. The security guard looked over at Cam and he nodded his head in a yes manner.

"So your man is a pig?" Cam asked with a hint of jealously in his voice. He hated the police and everything they stood for.

"Yes my boyfriend is a cop and please be nice," Bambi warned.

Cam watched as a muscular man in a police uniform enter into the studio. The first thing that Cam noticed was the arm full of tattoos and then the further he came into the studio, Cam recognized him. It was Richard, the same man he'd just got into a fist fight with over Yolanda about a week ago.

"What the fuck?" Cam said to himself as he watched Bambi slide into Richard's arms and kiss him like she wasn't just sucking Cam's dick a few minutes ago.

"Cam I would like to introduce you to my boyfriend Richard, Richard this is Cam, Cam, Richard" Bambi said innocently, introducing the two.

"Nice to meet you Cam. I've heard a lot about you," Richard said extending his hand as if this was the first time that the two were meeting.

"Likewise," Cam replied as he reluctantly shook Richard's hand. He didn't know what was going on, but he definitely planned on finding out. Something about this whole situation just didn't feel right.

"Look baby I got my contract," Bambi said smiling showing Richard the folder.

"That's wonderful baby," Richard said with a fake smile. "We have to get going so why don't you grab your things?"

"Okay give me one second I have to pee real quick," Bambi said then disappeared in the bathroom.

"What the fuck are you doing here!?" Cam growled once he was sure that Bambi was out of ear shot.

"I came to pick up my shorty," Richard said with a smile.

"What about Yolanda?"

"What about her?" Richard asked coldly.

All Cam could do was laugh. "I told Yolanda not to fuck with you."

"You broke her heart Cam and I was there to pick up the pieces," Richard laughed. "I broke her off some of this good dick and got that stupid bitch to give me a few gees so I could get into the real estate business, now I'm just waiting to take all her income tax money, and then I'm done with the bitch," he said as if Yolanda was nothing.

"You a greasy nigga," Cam said. He wanted to break Richard's face right then and there but it was too late. The damage had already been done. He caught Yolanda at a vulnerable time, took advantage of her, and it was nothing Cam could do about it. "So let me guess, you going to do Bambi like that too right? You're going to use her for what you can and then get rid of her too?"

"You got it all wrong playboy," Richard smiled. "Bambi is my soul mate and I would never do that to her." He glanced at the bathroom door when he heard the toilet flush. "But I promise if you try to fuck my girl in any way, shape, form, or fashion I'll make you regret it for the rest of your life."

"Sorry that Vodka was running through me," Bambi said smiling as she returned from the bathroom. She gave Cam a hug and then her and Richard made their exit.

Once Bambi was gone Cam thought about how stupid Yolanda was for falling for a creep like Richard so quickly. Part of him wanted Yolanda to take a hit so he could say I told you so, but the other part of him didn't want to see Yolanda get hurt or caught up in no dumb shit. He picked up the phone and quickly dialed Yolanda's number. It rung a few times and then the voicemail picked up. He quickly hung up and called back again only to get the same result. "Fuck!" he cursed out of frustration.

Cam closed up the studio and planned on heading to the liquor store. Right now he could really use a drink. He still couldn't believe that Richard was playing both Bambi and Yolanda for a fool at the same time. He had to figure out some way to stop this before things got too far out of hand.

Cam stepped foot outside along with one of his security guards and quickly got tackled down to the ground as several gunshots filled the quiet streets with noise. Seconds later the sound of tires screeching could be heard as the hooptie drove recklessly down the street.

"What the fuck," Cam said to himself as he held his .380 in his hand and jogged over to his Benz. Someone was trying to kill him and everyone affiliated with him and he had no clue why. All he knew was from now on he would have to be more cautious and stay on point.

"SAME OLE SHIT"

Honey laid across the king sized bed with a serious attitude. It was 1:05 a.m. and Cam still hadn't made it back home yet. To make matters worse, he wasn't answering his phone as usual. All kind of ugly thoughts ran through Honey's mind. If she had to guess, he was probably out spending Valentine's Day with the next chick, doing God only knows what with a complete stranger. Seconds later, the bedroom door pushed open and in walked Cam with an exhausted look on his face.

"Whatever your excuse is, I don't even want to hear it," Honey said not giving Cam a chance to speak. "Every time I call myself believing in you and giving you another chance you do this shit to me and every time I forgive you and take your trifling ass back, but not this time motherfucker!"

"Yes baby," Cam said and removed his clothes and headed for the shower.

Honey jumped up off the bed and blocked the entrance to the bathroom denying Cam access. "I knooooooow you don't think you just going to jump in the shower after being gone all day on Valentine's Day," she huffed looking at Cam like he had lost his mind.

"What? I can't take a shower?" Cam asked. "I need permission from you to take a shower now?"

"You trying to be funny?" Honey asked getting all up in Cam's face. Off of instinct he grabbed Honey's wrist so she couldn't hit him. Lately the two's relationship was becoming a physical one.

"Baby I just had a long day today," Cam huffed. "Not to mention someone tried to kill me."

"What? You're kidding right?" Honey asked with a nervous look on her face. She knew that there was a killer out there targeting all of Cam's love ones.

"Yeah some clown shot up the lobby of the studio," Cam shrugged as if someone trying to take his life was no big deal.

"That's why you need to pick up the phone when I'm calling because I be worried about you!" Honey snapped with her worry quickly turning into anger.

"I'm okay baby."

"How did things go with Bambi?" Honey asked with a raised brow. She could only imagine what type of foolishness had taken place in the studio.

"I don't want to talk about that," Cam said brushing her question off. "I missed you."

Not wanting to fuss or fight Honey decided to just leave it alone. "I missed you too baby."

Cam looked at Honey like she was insane. "Oh you thought I was talking about you?"

"Well if you're not talking about me, then who the fuck are you talking about?" Honey snapped with her hands on her hips.

"Her," Cam said looking down at Honey's freshly waxed pussy. He walked Honey back into the bathroom and helped her up on top of the sink. Honey rested her head back against the mirror and spread her legs wide open. She watched Cam burry his head in between her legs.

"Damn!" Honey moaned. The loud moaning, and slurping that came from between her legs drove her crazy. Honey grabbed the back of Cam's head and pushed it further into her pussy as she gyrated her hips in a circular motion. She wrapped her legs around Cam's head and squeezed his head tightly with her thighs as her orgasm threatened to spill. "Oh shit! Oh shit!"

Honey began shaking and bucking uncontrollably as her orgasm took over.

Cam stood up and jammed his dick inside of Honey's soaking wet box and tried to pulverize her insides. He had her hemmed up on the sink, with his hand wrapped around her throat while he was fucking the life out of her. When Cam was finished with Honey, she curled up on the bed and went straight to sleep like a baby. While Honey slept, Cam sat at the edge of the bed. He was racking his brain trying to figure out who would want him dead. His thoughts were interrupted when he heard his cell phone ring. He looked down at the screen and saw Yolanda's name flashing across the screen. "Yeah?"

"Cam please get over here quick! It's an emergency!!!!" Yolanda screamed into the phone and then the line went dead.

"Shit!" Cam shot up off the bed and headed out the door straight for Yolanda's house.

"YOU KNOW WHAT IT IS!"

Yolanda stood over the stove frying some chicken wings and making some rice. She knew Richard would be arriving within the next thirty minutes and she wanted his food to be fresh and hot when he showed up. Yolanda was really starting to fall in love with Richard. She loved everything about him down to the way he walked. Like clock work Yolanda heard a key in the lock followed by the door opening.

"Hey baby you're right on time. I was just..." Yolanda's words got caught in her throat when she saw a masked man holding

Richard in a choke hold with a gun pointed to his head. Seconds later a second gunman entered the house carrying a shotgun in his hand. He dramatically cocked a round into the chamber for extra emphasis.

"Where the fuck is the money!?" The second gunman barked.

Not knowing what to do Yolanda stood frozen like a deer trapped in the head lights.

"Baby please do what they say," Richard said with a scared look on his face. "Give them the money."

Yolanda nodded her head up and down and led the second gunman upstairs to the safe that was in the bedroom. Inside the safe rested about $250,000. Cam had left that money there in case of an emergency. Yolanda cracked open the safe and moved out of the way as she watched the the gunman snatch a pillow from off the bed and remove the pillow case and fill it with money. Once he was done, he roughly forced Yolanda back down stairs and made her and Richard get down on their knees and count to a hundred facing the wall, as they made their exit.

Richard allowed a few seconds to pass and then hopped up to his feet once he was sure that the gunmen were gone. He quickly ran into the kitchen and grabbed a knife from off the rack and ran out the door after the gunmen.

"Richard noooooo!" Yolanda screamed at the top of her lungs as she watched the love of her life run out the door with a knife in his hand. Not knowing what else to do, Yolanda ran and grabbed her cell phone and dialed Cam's number.

***

Richard ran out the front door just in time to see a burgundy van bend the corner. Without thinking twice Richard ran full speed after the van and when he reached the corner he spotted the van sitting idly at the end of the block. Richard ran up to the driver side window of the van and stuck his head inside. "Hey baby."

"Hey baby," Bambi said sitting behind the wheel of the burgundy van with a smile on her face. In the back of the van sat her two brothers who still wore their ski mask.

"Didn't I tell you that, that shit was going to be like taking candy from a baby?" Richard leaned in and kissed Bambi on her lips.

Bambi looked down at his hand and chuckled. "What the fuck was you going to do with that knife?"

"Shit, I had to make it look good," was Richard's response. "I love you baby and I'll see you at the house in a few hours," Richard said as he headed back to the house. He turned the corner and saw Yolanda standing outside in front of the house talking to a police officer with a scared look on her face. When she spotted him, she took off running in his direction and jumped into his arms.

"Oh my God! I was so worried about you," Yolanda said trying to squeeze the life out of Richard.

"They were in a silver van," Richard lied. "I tried to catch them, but I was a little too slow," he said as if he was sad about not being able to catch the bad guys.

"Baby please don't ever do that again!" Yolanda cried. "That was dangerous and stupid and you could have gotten yourself killed!"

"Sorry baby I was just trying to protect you," Richard said laying it on thick. "How much money did they get *us* for?"

"$250,000," Yolanda shrugged.

"Damn baby that's a lot of money."

"Wasn't my money. It was Cam's money," Yolanda said as if the robbery was no big deal because it wasn't her money.

"He gonna be mad at you."

"I could care less if Cam is mad or not," Yolanda said with an attitude. "That money saved your life and that's all that matters."

***

Cam pulled up to the house and saw flashing police lights everywhere. He quickly hopped out the car and jogged over to where he saw Yolanda standing on the front lawn. "What happened?"

"Two men showed up with guns and robbed us," Yolanda said wiping tears from her eyes.

"Us?" Cam echoed.

"Yeah me and Richard," Yolanda said nodding towards Richard who stood over to the side talking to a police officer. Right then and there Cam knew something wasn't right.

"What did they take from the house?" Cam asked.

"They took the money from the safe," Yolanda told him.

"I know you didn't give them niggaz all the money out of *my* safe," Cam said with fire dancing in his eyes.

"What was I supposed to do? They had a gun to Richard's head," Yolanda said as if that was a good enough reason to hand the gunmen Cam's money.

"Are you retarded?!" Cam yelled. "Use your brain!" he yelled jamming his index finger into Yolanda's forehead. "How many people knew about the safe?"

"Me, you, and Richard," Yolanda answered.

"Okay so you know I didn't rob you and you didn't rob yourself, so that only leaves one person," Cam pointed out.

"No," Yolanda shook her head. "Richard would never do that."

Cam gave Yolanda a sad look. "You want to be loved that bad that you can't even see when somebody is stealing from you?"

"You're just jealous," Yolanda capped back. That's what her mouth said, but she was really starting to consider what Cam was saying. The only people who did know about the safe were them three.

"Open your eyes!" Cam yelled. "This nigga is playing you for a fucking fool! You're smarter than that! Start using your head for more than just a ponytail!" Just as the words left Cam's mouth, Richard strolled over to where they were standing.

"Baby are you okay?" he asked Yolanda, but his focus was on Cam.

"Listen motherfucker!" Cam began. "If you wanna play her then that's fine, but when it comes to my money, that's where we have a problem!"

"What are you talking about?" Richard asked faking ignorance.

Cam sucked his teeth, turned, and stole on Richard. The punch caught Richard off guard causing him to stumble a few feet back. Cam quickly followed up with a series of left and right hooks to the head until two police officers roughly tackled Cam down to the ground and cuffed him. "That's word to my mother, I'mma kill you!" Cam shouted as the police officers dragged him away kicking and screaming.

Yolanda watched as the police officers dragged Cam away and immediately she began processing everything that he had been saying. She glanced over at Richard and something about the story just didn't seem right. "Fuck that I'm going to get to the bottom of this," Yolanda said to herself and then headed inside the house.

"THE NIGHT LIFE"

C am stepped foot out of the precinct and hopped in the passenger seat of the snow white Benz that sat curb side awaiting his arrival. He slid down into the passenger seat and Honey smoothly pulled out into traffic. "Which one of your bitches done got you in jail this time?" she asked with an attitude.

Cam ignored her and said nothing. He already knew before he even got into the car that Honey would have some slick shit to say and at the moment he had too much shit on his mind to be going back and forth with Honey over some dumb shit.

"Oh so you ain't got shit to say!?" Honey snapped. "I gotta get up out of my warm bed to come get your black ass out of jail and you just going to sit there and not say shit?"

"What do you want me to say?" Cam asked.

"Shit you can say something!"

"Just take me home so I can get dressed," Cam said waving Honey off.

"Oh you not spending time with me tonight?" Honey asked just looking for trouble. "I get out my warm bed to get you and now you can't spend time with me tonight?" she fussed. "We always busy so the one night when we get a night off you don't want to spend it with me?"

"I got business to take care of," Cam said quickly.

"What kind of business you gotta take care of?" Honey asked nosily. She didn't trust Cam one bit.

"I have to go to the club tonight. Bambi got a walk through. It's time to start getting her face out there."

"Okay what time are *we* going to the club?" Honey asked glancing over at Cam.

"*We* ain't going nowhere. I'm going to the club and you're going to get back in your warm bed," Cam told her. When they made it back to the house, Honey asked Cam a million and one questions and threatened to kill Cam and Bambi if she found out any bullshit was going on. It took Cam two hours to finally get dressed and get Honey up off of his back.

"I would like for you to invite Bambi over for dinner tomorrow night," Honey suggested. "If we all are going to be working together, then I think it's best that we all sit down and get to know one another a little better, plus I need to meet the bitch that's going to be spending a whole bunch of time with my man."

"Fine; dinner tomorrow night," Cam agreed as he rushed out the door. He knew if he didn't agree that him and Honey would be fighting and arguing about it all night so he decided to take the high road and agree just to keep the peace.

"SURPRISE, SURPRISE"

Marcus sat on the couch in his one bedroom apartment with his hand down his pants and the laptop sitting on the coffee table. On the laptop screen was a porno. The video was of some big booty black chick with a whole bunch of baby oil covering her body. She screamed and moaned loudly as a big rough looking dude pounded her from the back with no remorse.

Marcus sat on the couch jerking off to the video when the front door came crashing open. Marcus jumped when he saw the front door get kicked open. Seconds later, two masked men entered the apartment. The taller gunman held a Dessert Eagle in his hand, while the shorter gunman held a shiny hunting knife in his hand.

"Hey fellas," Marcus said in a nervous tone with his hands up in the air in surrender. "I think ya'll may have the wrong house."

The tall gunman walked over and slapped Marcus across the face with the Dessert Eagle sending blood splattering against the wall.

"What do you guys want I don't have any money?" Marcus asked holding his bloody mouth.

The short gunman ran up to Marcus and jammed the knife in and out of his chest repeatedly. He then ran the sharp blade across his throat for good measure. Once that was done, the tall gunman walked up and emptied his clip in Marcus' already dead body. The gunmen stared down at Marcus's dead body for a few seconds before they made their exit.

"DINNER"

Bambi laid on the hotel room bed on all fours with her face buried into the white pillow. She may have been out to scam Cam and take all of his money, but she had to admit that he had some good dick that she was starting to get addicted to. Cam spread Bambi's ass cheeks apart as he rammed his dick in and out of her wetness. He took pride bringing pleasure to women. Cam watched as Bambi's ass jiggled and slapped against his torso with each stroke he delivered. He smiled as Bambi's legs began to shake and she came all over his dick.

Cam quickly spun Bambi around and shoved his dick into her mouth and watched as she hungrily sucked as he thrust in and out of her mouth. He held onto her head to keep it still.

"Shit!" Cam growled as he came and felt Bambi swallowing. Bambi sucked the life out of Cam's dick and she didn't stop until he had to forcefully remove her mouth from his dick. "Damn! It ain't no more," he joked.

Bambi wiped the sides of her mouth with her hand and then smiled. "Had to make sure I got it all out."

Cam and Bambi took a shower together where round two took place. Once they were done, they quickly got dressed, exited the hotel, and hopped in Cam's Benz.

"You think Honey is going to like me?" Bambi asked. She had been nervous ever since Cam had told her about the dinner. She had no idea what to expect.

"Everything is going to be fine," Cam replied. But the truth of the matter was, he didn't know what to expect and with Honey one could never tell. Cam just hoped and prayed that when they got there Honey hadn't already been drinking.

Cam pulled into the driveway and killed the engine. "Relax everything is going to be fine," Cam told her.

"Nigga please I'm about to fuck you and Honey's whole world up," Bambi said to herself as she stepped out of the car and followed Cam inside the mansion. She hated men like Cam who felt that he could have his cake and eat it too just because he had money. Bambi planned on teaching him a lesson that he would never forget.

"Well it's about time you two showed up," Honey said. "I thought for a second ya'll might had gotten lost," she said slyly as she looked Bambi up and down and she wasn't impressed.

Immediately Cam recognized that Honey had been drinking and knew that the night would definitely be very eventful.

Cam, Bambi, Honey, and Truck all sat down and enjoyed a nice dinner that the chef had whipped up.

"So how did you and Cam meet?" Bambi asked breaking the silence.

Honey took a sip of her wine as she stared a hole in Bambi. "A better question is, what do *you* want from Cam?" she asked flipping the script.

Truck secretly looked at Cam and shook his head. He already knew how this was going to end.

"I want the same thing from Cam that you want," Bambi answered with a smile.

"And that is?"

"Him to manage me and bring success to my career," Bambi said winking at Honey.

Honey wanted to hop across the table and whip Bambi's ass, but she did her best to remain calm. "You think you have what it takes to be a super star?"

"Absolutely! Don't you?" Bambi asked. All eyes at the table landed on Honey awaiting her response.

"I mean," Honey began. "I guess we can put some make-up on you and cop you a few sleezy outfits. I heard slut is in nowadays."

Bambi took a sip of her wine and smiled. "Do you feel threatened by my presence?"

Honey chuckled. "Let me explain something to you sweety. I'll never be threatened by the help. You can try to sing like me, dress like me, and even act like me, but the fact still remains you'll never be me, hoe!"

"Did Cam tell you that we just got finished fucking before we came here?" Bambi asked. The look on Honey's face told Bambi that she had just crushed her with that last question.

Honey looked over at Cam. "Is this true?" Cam's silence was all the answer that Honey needed. She chuckled and took a sip from her wine as she discreetly removed her shoes under the table. With the quickness of a rattle snake, Honey jumped across the table and tackled Bambi out of the chair. She landed on top of Bambi and rained punch after punch down onto Bambi's exposed face until Cam and Truck quickly got her up off of Bambi.

Bambi stood to her feet with her face covered in blood and smiled. "You stupid ass bitch! That's just what I wanted! Now I'm going to sue the shit out of your stupid ass!" she yelled as she hurled her wine glass at Honey.

Cam roughly grabbed Bambi by her arm and snatched her outside. "What the fuck was that all about!?"

"It's about you having a girl and you still fucking me as if you were single," Bambi said with a bloody smile. "But you done fucked with the wrong one this time!"

"Fuck is you talking about?" Cam asked with a confused look on his face.

"Before you ran up in me raw, did you ever even take the time to ask me if I was clean?"

"What are you saying?

"I have HIV Cam," Bambi said with a bloody smile. "And guess what? Now so do you!"

After the words left Bambi's lips, Cam blacked out and wrapped his hands around her neck and proceeded to squeeze the life out of her. Bambi's eyes rolled back into her head as she gasped for air. She scratched at Cam's hands hoping that he'd release his grip.

"That's enough!!!" Truck yelled as he ran outside and pried Cam's hands from around Bambi's neck. Once Cam's grip was released, Bambi coughed, got up, and took off running.

"Cam you gotta chill," Truck said as he helped escort Cam back inside the house. As soon as Cam stepped foot in the house, Honey blasted him across his face with two powerful punches that stumbled him and gave him an instant headache. Cam took the punches like a champ as he walked over to the table, sat down, and buried his face in his hands.

Honey was getting ready to grab the wine bottle and crack Cam over his head with it, but she stopped short when she heard him crying. Out of all the years that she had known him, she had never seen or heard Cam cry. Cam sat at the table crying his eyes out like a baby.

"Boss you alright?" Truck asked with a look of concern on his face. Cam said nothing. Instead he just continued to cry.

"We going to be okay," Honey said squatting down and removing Cam's hands from his face so she could look at him.

"No we're not!" Cam cried. "Bambi just told me that she has HIV!"

Honey took a moment to allow her brain to process the information that she had just received. "You had sex with her raw Cam?"

Cam nodded his head yes. "I'm sorry."

Honey looked Cam in his eyes. "I promise we'll get through this the same way we get through everything else and you know how that is?"

"Together," Cam whispered. Honey pulled him in and hugged him tightly. Cam may have been a lot of fucked up things, but the fact still remained that he was still all hers. "They say you can't help who you love and Cam I love you no matter what!"

"I love you too baby and I'm sorry" Cam said. He hated that he had to learn the hard way that all he really needed was one strong woman who would stay in his corner through thick and thin.

"Look at me Cam," Honey grabbed Cam's face with both hands forcing him to face her. "It's me and you forever now do you understand?"

Cam nodded his head yes.

"No I need to hear you say it!"

"It's me and you forever!" Cam said as he got up and headed for the door. It had just dawned on him that if Bambi had HIV, then so did Richard, and if Richard had it then that meant that Yolanda also had it.

"Where you going?" Honey asked.

"Yolanda was fooling around with some guy that was messing with Bambi and I have to go over there and tell her to get herself checked out. I need to give her the heads up."

"Okay be careful baby," Honey said as she watched Cam storm out the front door.

"YOU RE A MONSTER"

For the past few days, Yolanda had been giving what Cam said some thought and ever since then she started paying attention to small details. She was starting to see that Richard wasn't who he said he was. For the past few days, Yolanda had been following Richard around and she found out that he was living a double life with another woman. She watched him kiss, hug, and interact with another woman the same way that he had been doing with her. What pissed Yolanda off the most was the fact that Richard had played her for a fool after she had told him all about the shit that Cam had put her through.

Yolanda sat parked outside Richard's other woman's house and at the moment the both of them were currently inside together.

Yolanda took a deep breath and hopped out of the car and headed to the front door to confront Richard. On the count of three Yolanda knocked on the door and patiently waited for someone to answer. Seconds later a beautiful woman answered the door. She was barefoot and she wore a sports bra and a pair of boy shorts.

"Can I help you?" the woman asked.

"Yes, your name please?" Yolanda immediately got an attitude when she thought of the beautiful woman doing all sorts of nasty things with her man.

"I'm Bambi," the woman said smiling. "And you must be Yolanda right?"

"How did you know?"

"Baby your little girlfriend is here!" Bambi yelled stepping to the side so Yolanda could enter the house.

Richard came around the corner, looked at Yolanda, and nonchalantly said, "Hey."

"Hey?" Yolanda repeated. "That's all you have to say is *hey*?"

"What do you want?" Richard asked coldly. He couldn't wait to see the look on Yolanda's face when he dropped the bomb on her.

"For starters, an explanation would be nice," Yolanda said with her hands on her hips.

"Listen Yolanda, I used you and took advantage of you. I never loved you and I never will," Richard told her. "Oh and I have HIV," he said with a smile as if he had just told a joke.

Yolanda's mouth hung open in shock as her brain processed what Richard had just told her. Before she realized what had happened, her hand balled up into a fist and shot out and punched Richard in the mouth. Yolanda went to charge Richard and scratch his eyes out, but out of nowhere Bambi caught her with a sucker punch to the side of her face that put her down.

"Bitch!" Richard growled as he roughly grabbed Yolanda by the collar of her shirt and roughly escorted her over to the front door, where he dramatically tossed Yolanda out the door head first not caring where she landed. Richard slammed the door as him and Bambi broke out into a laughing fit. Richard and Bambi were just two people who had gotten dealt a bad hand in life and got the HIV virus and out of spite they decided to pass the virus on to as many people as they could.

"Did you see the look on that bitch face when you told her that you had HIV?" Bambi asked laughing. Her laughter quickly came to an end when the front door came crashing open and in the doorway stood two masked men dressed in all black. The taller of the two gunmen held a dessert eagle while the other man held a sharp hunting knife.

"Something funny!?" the shorter masked man asked closing the door behind him. "I wanna laugh too."

"Listen Yolanda if that's you, this isn't funny," Richard said in a shaky tone.

"Who's Yolanda?" the masked man asked chuckling.

Without warning the taller gunman aimed the gun at Richard's leg and pulled the trigger.

BOOM!

Everyone watched as Richard went down quick and hard. The gunman then trained his gun on Bambi and shot her in the leg too.

BOOM!

The shorter gunman then kneeled down over Richard and jammed the hunting knife down into his stomach repeatedly. The masked man raised the knife high and then came down hard with each thrust until Richard was dead. The taller masked man then stepped up and put a bullet in Richard's head for good measure.

The shorter masked man then made his way over to where Bambi laid and stood over her. "So you like to give people HIV right?" Before Bambi could reply, the masked man jammed the knife down into the pit of her stomach and gave the handle a nice strong twist. As Bambi felt the life exiting her body she reached up and snatched the mask off of her attackers head. "Oh my God it's you," she gasped as the masked man stabbed her repeatedly until she was no longer breathing. The masked man quickly grabbed his mask from off the floor and slipped it back on his head as the taller masked man walked over and put a bullet in Bambi's head silencing her forever.

"WTF"

C am pulled up in front of Yolanda's house as the rain began to pour down. "Fuck!" Cam growled. He hated the rain. The bomb shell that Bambi had dropped on him earlier still weighed heavy on his mind. As beautiful as Bambi was, he would have never expected her to have the HIV virus. Cam hopped out of his Benz and ran up to the front door. He got ready to ring the doorbell until he saw that the front door was already slightly ajar. Cam entered the house and found Yolanda sitting on the couch with her face buried in her hands as she cried her eyes out.

"Looks like you could use some company," Cam said letting Yolanda know that she was no longer in the house alone.

Yolanda looked up and saw Cam standing there. "I have HIV Cam."

Cam chuckled. "Yeah me too."

Yolanda stood to her feet. "You think this shit is funny? This all your fault!"

"How is this all my fault?" Cam asked.

"Because if you would have just done right when we were together, we would be living happily ever after right now, but no you just had to go out and fuck all these other women!" Yolanda cried.

Cam thought about it for a second and Yolanda had a good point. If he could go back and change a few things, he would do it in a heartbeat. "I'm sorry baby. I never meant for all of this to happen."

"I hate you Cam! You ruined my entire life!" Yolanda said through clench teeth as she punched him in his chest. "Get the fuck out of my life forever!"

The sound of the front door getting kicked open grabbed both of their attention. Seconds later two masked men entered through the front door soaking wet. Before Cam could even say a word he watched as the taller masked man shot Yolanda in the leg.

Yolanda looked up from the floor crying, looking at Cam for him to help her, but instead he stood frozen like a deer caught in headlights. "Please Cam help me... Pllllease..." Yolanda's cries ended when the shorter gunman stabbed her like she was an animal out in the wilderness. He then stood up and stared Cam in the face before he removed his mask.

Cam frowned when he saw who the masked man was. "Honey what the fuck are you doing?"

"It's funny that I would find you here," Honey said still holding the knife in her hand.

"So you've been the one killing everyone?"

"The problem is that you get distracted too easily. So I had to remove all of the distractions," Honey told him as she walked over to the fridge and grabbed an open bottle of wine and guzzled straight from the bottle. "Now because of you I have HIV. How do you plan on fixing that?"

"Whatever you need me to do I got you," Cam said seriously.

"Truck you heard that right?" Honey asked. Truck removed his mask and said, "Yeah I heard him."

"You was in on this too Truck?" Cam asked in disbelief. He was convinced that the two of them were officially crazy.

"She's the boss," Truck said with a smile. "I just follow orders."

"Cam you gave me HIV" Honey reminded him. "You basically took my life, so what I'm going to do is give you two options," she paused for a second. "One I can kill you right now or two you can be with me and only me and ride this thing out with me and only me... What's it going to be?"

Cam pulled Honey in close for a hug. "I love you and we going to work this out."

Honey smiled as she dropped the knife and slid down to one knee and pulled out a ring. "Cam will you marry me?"

Cam looked over at Yolanda's dead body and then looked down at the crazed look on Honey's face. "Yes baby I'll marry you," he said placing a fake smile on his face.

"This bitch is crazy and I'm going to have to find a way to get away from this crazy bitch before she kills me in my sleep," Cam said to himself as he acted as if everything was fine.

"Cam if you ever cheat on me again I promise I will kill you," Honey told him with a serious look on her face. "Promise me now that you'll never cheat on me ever again."

"I promise I'll never cheat on you again," Cam said.

"THREE YEARS LATER."

C am sat on the couch playing Madden. For the past two years he hadn't even looked at another woman. This was the longest that he'd been faithful in his life and he had to admit that it wasn't that bad being with just one woman and one woman only. Honey had turned back into her old self and she showed no signs of turning back into a ruthless killer. Cam really didn't trust Truck or want him in the house but he just kept quiet to prevent problems.

"Daddy, daddy I wanna play," Lil Cam whined as he reached for his controller. In order to keep his life Cam had to become an official family man. He'd been forced to get Honey pregnant shortly after they'd gotten married.

Honey came downstairs and kissed Cam on the cheek. "Fish for dinner tonight?"

"Nah I think I want to go out and eat tonight," Cam said as he followed Honey into the kitchen and palmed her ass and planted soft kisses on her neck. Cam slipped his hand down the front of her thong and began massaging her fat swollen clit.

"Oooww" Honey moaned. "Don't start anything you can't finish."

Just as Cam got ready to reply, he heard the doorbell ring. "Damn perfect timing," he said as he kissed Honey and went to go answer the door.

Cam opened the door and saw a white women standing on the other side of the door and by her side stood a young boy who couldn't have been no older than four years old. "Can I help you?"

"Hey Cam," the white girl said with a smile.

"I'm sorry have we met before," Cam said playing dumb. The white girl that stood before him was one of his old side chicks that he used to deal with years ago, but her mother had gotten sick so she had to leave town to go and take care of her mother and that was the last time Cam had seen her.

"Stop playing Cam," the white girl said. "Sorry. I didn't mean to just pop up at your house like this, but I didn't have no other way to get in touch with you."

"Well thanks for stopping by Amanda, but now isn't the best time," Cam said in a rushed tone. "Give me your number and I'll call you later."

"Okay but first I would like for you to meet somebody," Amanda said with a smile. "I would like to introduce you to your son. David this is your father Camron, Camron meet David."

"Hey dad," little David said shyly.

Before Cam could find the words to reply, Honey walked up nosily and looked the white girl up and down.

"Hi you doing? Can I help you?" Honey asked in a professional manner.

TO BE CONTINUED...

Books by Good2Go Authors on Our Bookshelf

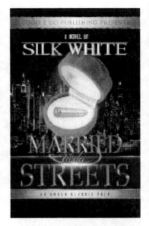

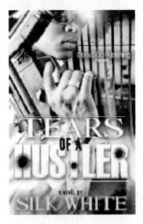

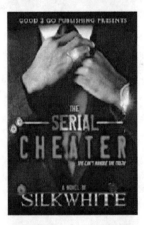

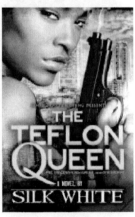

Good2Go Films Presents